Tiger Town

Other Tiger Titles by Eric Walters

Also by Eric Walters

Tiger Town

Eric Walters

A SANDCASTLE BOOK
A MEMBER OF THE DUNDURN GROUP
TORONTO

Editor: Jen Hamilton
Production and Design: Jen Hamilton
Cover Art: Ron Lightburn
Author Photograph: Paula Esplen

Library and Archives Canada Cataloguing in Publication

Walters, Eric, 1957-

  Tiger town / Eric Walters.

ISBN-10: 1-55002-631-3
ISBN-13: 978-1-55002-631-3

  I. Title.

PS8595.A598T587 2006   jC813'.54   C2006-902681-5

Conseil des Arts
du Canada

Canada Council
for the Arts

Canada

ONTARIO ARTS COUNCIL
CONSEIL DES ARTS DE L'ONTARIO

We acknowledge the support of the Canada Council for the Arts and the Ontario Arts Council for our publishing program. We also acknowledge the financial support of the Government of Canada through the Book Publishing Industry Development Program and The Association for the Export of Canadian Books, and the Government of Ontario through the Ontario Book Publishers Tax Credit program, and the Ontario Media Development Corporation.

Care has been taken to trace the ownership of copyright material used in this book. The author and the publisher welcome any information enabling them to rectify any references or credits in subsequent editions.
                                                                                        J. Kirk Howard, President

Printed and bound in Canada by Friesens
www.dundurn.com

Dundurn Press
3 Church Street, Suite 500
Toronto, Ontario, Canada
M5E 1M2

Gazelle Book Services Limited
White Cross Mills
High Town, Lancaster, England
LA1 4XS

Dundurn Press
2250 Military Road
Tonawanda, NY,
U.S.A. 14150

For my wife, Anita

Chapter 1

I awoke with a start. What was that noise? It had been real... hadn't it? Or was it just something I'd thought I'd heard in my dreams? It was hard enough for me to sleep in my own house, with its own noises, but it was always harder at somebody else's place. My sleep had been so disturbed that I'd already woken up a half-dozen times and—there it was again! It sounded like something dragging across the floor. My mind raced to all the horror movies I'd seen. The one scene that stuck was that of a body being dragged across the floor. That was what it sounded like.

"Smarten up," I said to myself softly. Sometimes my imagination got the better of me. This wasn't a horror movie, and there was no body. This was Mr. McCurdy's farmhouse, and there was nothing here to be afraid of. Of course, that didn't stop me from wishing that my mother was here. Maybe our house was just the next farm over, across a few fields, but it might as well have been on the other side of the country for all the good it was doing me now.

At least I had Nick. He was sleeping in a room down the hall. Though somehow relying on my eleven-year-old brother for protection wasn't a particularly reassuring thought.

I pulled my feet out from under the covers, threw them to the side, and stood. The floor creaked and groaned under my weight. I began to shuffle across the floor as quietly as I could. I reached the door and peered down the darkened hall. I couldn't see anything. Fumbling along the wall, I tried to locate the light switch. It couldn't be far away. I was sure it was—my hand bumped into the face plate, and I flipped the switch. There was a quiet click, but no light. Oh, right, this one didn't work. The wiring in this house was as old as the house itself, and many of the switches didn't work. I'd had to turn the hall light off from the kitchen when I shut everything down last night.

Maybe I should just retreat into my room. I could turn on the lamp beside my bed to throw a little light down the hall. Then again, maybe it was better if I didn't turn on the light. The dark didn't just stop me from seeing, but stopped anybody from seeing me. Somehow, being in the dark seemed safe, or at least safer.

The noise came again. It wasn't so much a dragging sound as something being pushed. It reminded me of the noise a chair makes when you get up from your desk at school.

There's nothing to be afraid of, I thought. *Don't be stupid. Just walk down the hall.* It was nothing. Certainly not something to be afraid of. Certainly not someone dragging a body around. Or pushing it. Could you even push a body?

I pressed my body tightly against the wall and started to slide down the hall. This was a trick my brother had shown me that minimized the creaking of the floorboards when you moved around in old houses like ours—or Mr. McCurdy's. Slowly I inched toward the kitchen. I knew there was nothing to fear, but my head didn't seem to be winning the argument with my body; my knees were shaking, my stomach fluttering, my mouth was dry, and the hairs on the back of my neck were all standing at attention.

I had never liked the dark and was still spooked by our farmhouse with its nooks and crannies. It was even worse at Mr. McCurdy's place in the dead—*the middle*—of the night. Why had I even volunteered to stay here with Nick while Mr. McCurdy was away? I knew somebody had to watch the animals, but it didn't have to be just us. Our mother had said she'd stay with us, but she didn't sleep well unless she was in her bed, and she was preparing for a big trial at work and needed all the rest she could get. Besides, I was fourteen years old—a very grown-up fourteen-year-old—and I didn't need to be baby-sat while I was baby-sitting.

Of course, as I stood there in my bare feet, in my pajamas, in the dark, in the middle of the night, in Mr. McCurdy's house, I wouldn't have minded having my mother there beside me. I couldn't even call her. Mr. McCurdy's phone was dead, or rather, disconnected. He hadn't had a working phone since before we met him.

The sound came again. Somebody was moving around in the kitchen. It had to be Nick. Probably fixing himself a snack—that kid was always hungry. But why wouldn't he have turned on the kitchen light? It would be awfully hard to fix a sandwich in the dark.

I stood and listened as the noises continued. They were louder, closer, clearer, coming from the kitchen, the *dark* kitchen, right on the other side of the wall I was pressed against. I stood frozen, not able to move forward, but not wanting to go back. I couldn't just stand here all night, though, could I? I wondered what time it was, and how many hours until the sunrise when the kitchen wouldn't be so dark. Hold on—I didn't have to wait until then to get light.

Slowly I moved my hand around the corner of the kitchen, feeling for the switch and…I touched another hand!

"Ahhhh!" I screamed as my hand was grabbed tightly and the light flicked on. I was dragged into the kitchen and—"Calvin!"

I was held tightly in the big hairy mitt of Calvin, Mr. McCurdy's pet chimpanzee. "You almost scared me to death!" I exclaimed breathlessly. Actually, until my heart settled back into my chest from my throat, I wasn't one hundred percent sure he hadn't.

"Can I please have my hand back?" I demanded.

Calvin reached down, gave my hand a big, wet, sloppy kiss,

and released it. *Ugggg*. I guess I couldn't complain. Sometimes he kissed me on the face, and chimps have just about the worst breath in the world.

"Sarah, are you okay?" Nick called out, running into the kitchen. He looked scared.

"I'm fine. I was just—"

"What the heck happened in here?"

I looked around. All the furniture—table, chairs, the buffet, the old couch—had been pushed to the far side of the kitchen. And each and every cupboard was wide open.

"Calvin, did you do this?" I asked.

He looked down at the floor and put his hands over his eyes.

"Did you, Calvin?" I asked louder.

"Sarah, do you really expect him to answer?" Nick questioned. "Who else do you think could have done it?"

"I guess you're right, but why would he move all the furniture?"

"Looks pretty obvious to me," Nick said.

"It isn't to me."

"He was looking for something to eat and climbed the furniture to get to the top cupboards. Look."

It was then I noticed Calvin hadn't just opened the cupboards, but had pulled everything out. The table was covered with jars and bottles and boxes, most open, some lying on their side, spilling and dripping their contents onto the floor.

"Calvin, you are a *bad* chimp!" I scolded. "You are a very, very bad chimp!"

Calvin took his hands off his eyes and placed them firmly over his ears.

"He's gone from 'see no evil' to 'hear no annoying sister!'" Nick laughed.

Calvin laughed with him. Apparently he could hear some things. Equally apparent was something I'd known for a long time: the ape and my brother shared the same sense of humour.

I grabbed Calvin by the hand, trying to pull him to his feet. He sat there, refusing to move. He was far too heavy and strong to be moved against his will.

"You have to clean up this mess!" I shouted.

Calvin took his free hand and put his thumb to his nose, spread his fingers, and went *"PPPPIlllllllffffffff,"* spraying spit into the air and my face!

"That's disgusting!" I said as I let go of him and wiped my face on the sleeve of my pajamas.

"Forget about a little monkey slobber," Nick said. "What's Mom going to say when she sees all this?"

"Oh, my gosh, you're right. She's going to go crazy. Calvin's got to clean this up."

"Sarah, think about what you're saying. Calvin's a chimpanzee. Chimpanzees are very good at *making* a mess, but not really good at *cleaning up* those messes. You're going to have to clean it up."

"If I'm going to be cleaning, so will you," I said.

"Me? Why should I clean up? I didn't make this mess."

"Neither did I!" I protested.

"Yeah, but I'm not the one in charge here. You are. Since you're in charge, you're the one who's responsible. And since you're responsible, you have to be the one who does the cleaning." He paused and smiled. "And could you try to keep it down? I want to go back to bed and get some sleep and—"

"You're not going anywhere!" I snapped, grabbing him by the arm as he started to walk away. Unlike the chimp, I easily spun him around. "I'm in charge of everything, including you. So you're going to work, too!"

Nick looked as if he was going to argue, but shut his mouth.

"What time is it?" I asked.

Nick glanced at his watch. "It's almost five in the morning."

"That gives us three hours to get this cleaned up before Mom drops in to check on us on her way to work. We have to get going."

"Well, at least we have some help," Nick said.

"We do?"

Nick walked over to one of the partially opened cupboards and pulled it the rest of the way open. Inside, his head buried deep within a bag of overturned cookies, was Polly, Mr. McCurdy's macaw.

"He's helping clean up the cookies!" Nick laughed.

"That's not helping!" I rushed over, reached up, and grabbed the bag of cookies, practically ripping it off Polly's head. He squawked loudly, dropping the partially eaten piece of Oreo he had in his beak. As I started to roll up the bag, he ruffled all his feathers.

"Stupid girl!" Polly exclaimed, and Nick burst into laughter again. It wasn't just the monkey who was on the same level as my brother.

"Be quiet, you stupid bird!" I yelled.

"Go home, ugly girl!" Polly squawked.

"Don't you tell me to—"

"Sarah, you're arguing with a bird," Nick said.

"Oh, yeah."

"Even worse, you were losing the argument," Nick snickered. "By the way, where's Laura?"

I'd forgotten about her. Laura was Mr. McCurdy's gentle old cheetah. She lived in the house, too. Cheetahs were the only big cats you could trust to live in your home—she wouldn't hurt a fly. She spent most of her time sleeping on the couch. The couch was spun around, facing away from me against the far wall under the cupboards. I walked over. There she was on the couch, on her back, her paws in the air, sound asleep, gently snoring.

"How could Laura sleep through all of that?" Nick asked.

"Mr. McCurdy says she's even more deaf than he is."

"Maybe he should get her a hearing aid."

"Right," I snorted. "I can see that happening—right after Mr. McCurdy gets one for himself."

"Sometimes I don't think he needs one," Nick said. "Ever notice how he hears everything he wants to hear?"

"I thought it was just me who'd noticed that."

"What's all over Laura?" Nick asked.

I looked down. Just by her back leg there was a patch of bright red! "She's bleeding! She's been hurt!"

Nick reached down and put a finger in the blood. Before I could react he popped it into his mouth! My mouth dropped open in shock and disgust.

"Jam." Nick reached over and grabbed a jar of jam that was sitting on its side with the top off. He sat it upright and licked his fingers again. "Strawberry jam."

"Nicholas, use a cloth!"

"Why, are you afraid I might make a mess?"

"We have to get started on this mess somewhere. Get started by washing your hands, and we'll go from there."

Nick shrugged and shambled over to the sink. I knew where I was going to start. I grabbed a dishcloth, rung it out, and walked back to Laura. Gently I began to dab at the patch of jam staining her fur. As I rubbed harder, one of Laura's eyes popped open.

"Hello, Laura," I said. With my free hand I scratched behind one of her ears. Cheetahs loved to be scratched there. Actually all cats, big or small, liked to have their ears rubbed.

"Sarah, what are you doing?" Nick asked.

"What does it look like I'm doing?"

"It looks like you're cleaning a cat."

"Yeah, so what?"

Nick shook his head sadly. "Remember how I said that chimps aren't good at cleaning up?"

"Yeah."

"Well, cats *are* good at cleaning...at least cleaning themselves. Watch." Again Nick dipped a finger into the jam on Laura's side. Then he put it in Laura's mouth. Her eyes opened wide, and she began licking his finger. He moved his hand away and her head followed, tongue darting out, down to her splattered leg. She began to lick the jam off her fur.

"Nick, I have to hand it to you," I said. "You are a genius—"

"Thank you."

"When it comes to avoiding work," I said, finishing my sentence. "If you were half as smart at doing work as you are at avoiding it, you'd be getting straight A's at school."

"Straight A's would be way too show-offy. I wouldn't want to be like that. Not like some people I know who love to show off."

"First of all, you couldn't get the marks I do, because I'm smart, and second, there's a big difference between being smart and being a smart-aleck…like some people I know," I taunted.

"I don't know," Nick said. "If you were really smart, you'd be a heck of a lot nicer to the only person who can help you clean up this mess."

Darn…he was right.

"Well?" Nick asked.

"Well, what?"

"Are you going to apologize?"

"To who?"

"To me. For insulting my intelligence."

"You want me to apologize?" I asked.

He nodded.

"You must be crazy if you think—"

"Now you have to apologize twice—once for calling me stupid, and once for calling me crazy."

"There's no way I'm going to apologize to you! What I'm going to do is tell Mom that you didn't listen to me!"

Nick smiled. "You won't do that."

"Why not?"

"Because if you tell Mom, she'll get mad at me."

"That's the idea," I said.

"And if she gets mad at me, she'll punish me."

"Again, that's the idea!"

"And the way she'll probably punish me is to make me stay home, and you'll be here tonight...all alone."

Nick's smile grew while my smirk first froze and then vanished. He had me, and he knew it. Even worse, he knew that I knew he knew it.

"Well," he said. "I'm still waiting."

It was bad enough being here with just Nick in the house. Without him it would be awful. And Mr. McCurdy wasn't due back for at least one more night. I swallowed hard. Twice. I took a deep breath. "I'm sorry," I mumbled.

"What did you say?" Nick asked. "I couldn't really hear you."

I felt myself getting hot. I opened my mouth and quickly closed it. There was no point in saying anything that would cost me a third apology.

"Nick, I am very, very sorry that I offended you in any way by implying that either your sanity or intelligence was in question."

"What? What does that mean?"

What it meant was that he was too stupid to understand what I'd just said. "It means that I'm sorry I said you were stupid or crazy."

"Oh, good," he replied. "In that case, I'll help."

Chapter 2

I put the mop away and looked at the finished result. The floor was clean. The table was clean. The counters were clean. The furniture was back in its regular place and the cupboards were properly organized. I didn't remember ever seeing Mr. McCurdy's kitchen this clean. Or, for that matter, any part of his house. Mr. McCurdy was a wonderful guy, but he wasn't much better at cleaning than Calvin was. His house always had more of a "lived-in" look—although it had certainly gotten better over the past year. Since we'd been coming around, I'd been helping to clean up sometimes.

"There, finished," I said proudly. "It looks perfect."

"Maybe *too* perfect," Nick replied.

"How can it look too perfect?"

"Personally I'd get suspicious if I saw anything that looked this clean. I'd wonder what was being hidden. Maybe we should mess it up a little."

"I don't think we have to worry about messing it up," I suggested. "Calvin will take care of that all by himself."

The chimp was sitting on the floor with his back against the cupboards, drinking his second can of Coke. The first, empty and crunched, was sitting on the floor beside him.

"You better put that in the garbage can," I warned him.

Calvin reached down and picked it up.

"See," I said to Nick, "he can be taught to be tidy."

Calvin wound up and whipped the can across the room. I ducked as it soared over my head and smacked into the wall right beside Polly. A flash of flustered feathers flew into the air, and he soared out of the room, squawking and swearing.

I gave Calvin a dirty look but didn't say anything. He shouldn't have thrown the can at Polly, but he hadn't hit him. Besides, there had been a couple of times when I wanted to toss something at that rude bird myself.

"Did you hear that?" Nick asked.

I turned to listen. It was the sound of gravel crunching underneath tires—it had to be Mom.

"What time is it?" I asked. My watch was still on the table beside my bed.

Nick looked at his wrist. "Almost nine."

"Nine! I didn't know it was that late. Mom was supposed to be here around eight. I wonder why she's so late?"

"Let's find out." Nick raced for the door and I hurried after him. He went through first, letting it slam shut with a loud thud. I pushed it open and skidded to a stop, bumping into Nick who stood just feet from the door. Why had he stopped? Then I saw the reason. The car coming up the driveway wasn't our mother's—it was a police cruiser!

Normally I didn't mind the police. That was, I didn't mind them anywhere except at Mr. McCurdy's farm. My few dealings with them here had always been a problem—things like the mayor ordering them to remove Mr. McCurdy's animals. Thank goodness that had all ended well.

"I wonder what the police want," Nick said.

"Probably nothing," I said, hoping I knew what I was talking about.

"Yeah, right, the cops are coming out here to say hello."

The car came to a halt. "I guess we won't have to wait long to find out."

The driver's door opened and out popped an officer. It was the captain! He was second in command of the whole police department. We'd first gotten to know him when Mr. McCurdy's tiger, Buddha, had escaped. He was a pretty decent guy, but he was still a police officer, and he made me more than a little nervous. He wouldn't be out here unless it was for something important.

The passenger door opened and—"Mom?"

"What's our mother doing in a police car?" Nick asked. He sounded as confused as I was.

"I don't know." I couldn't think of an explanation that was even remotely possible.

"You don't think she's been arrested, do you?" Nick asked.

"Of course not! Don't be ridiculous!"

"Sarah! Nicholas!" she yelled as she came toward us, waving a hand in the air. She gave us both a big hug. "I want you to know that I'm all right," she said in a serious voice.

A bolt of electricity shot up my spine. "What do you mean you're all right? Why wouldn't you be all right? What happened?" I demanded.

"Nothing, nothing really."

"It must have been something, or you wouldn't have said you were all right!" I cried.

"Sarah, it was just a little accident."

"What sort of accident?"

"It was nothing...just a little car accident."

"Oh, my gosh! A car accident! That's awful, are you injured? Are you—"

"Sarah, she's fine...remember?" Nick said.

"How did it happen?" I asked.

"I drove the car into the ditch."

"How did you do that?" Nick asked.

"I was on my way here when a deer darted out in front of me. I slammed on the brakes and—"

"Did you hit it?" I asked.

"It's fine. I missed it."

"Both your mother and the deer were lucky," the captain said. "Deer get hit by cars all the time. Besides killing the deer, it can really damage the car."

"How's our car?" Nick asked.

"It sustained some damage," Mom said.

"But I thought you missed the deer?"

"I missed the deer, but I hit the ditch. It had to be towed to town to be repaired."

"That's where I got involved," the captain said. "I heard the call for the tow truck over the radio and I went out to investigate."

"And you arrested our mother?" Nick asked.

"Of course not!" Mom exclaimed.

"Then why are you in his car?"

"I mentioned that I had to come out here and check on the two of you before I went into town, and Martin offered to give me a ride."

"Martin?" Nick and I both asked in unison.

"That's my first name," the captain said. "I have a first name, you know."

"Of course…we knew you probably did…I mean, definitely… Captain."

"Actually you shouldn't call me captain anymore," he said.

"You want us to call you Martin?" I asked in amazement.

"From what I've just been told, I think that chief would be more appropriate," our mother said.

"Chief? You're in charge of things?"

He laughed. "You sound shocked. Don't you think I can run everything?"

"No! Yes! It's just I thought that old guy was the chief, and I was just—"

"I'm joking," he said, cutting me off.

"You were? You mean you're not the chief?" I asked.

"Oh, no, that I was serious about. I meant about giving you a hard time."

"Oh…sure."

"My daughter says I have to learn to smile more when I'm kidding around. She tells me I scare people," the acting chief said.

"I didn't know you had kids," Nick said.

"Just one. She's about your age. She lives with her mother a few hours away from here, so I don't get to see her as much as I'd like, mainly holidays and during the summer."

"Is she here now?" Nick asked.

"Actually she was for the first part of the summer, but she's headed back to her mother's now."

I guessed all that meant he was divorced or separated or something. I didn't want to talk about any of that stuff. It had been almost two years since our parents separated, but it was still too close to the surface.

"What happened to the old chief?" I asked, changing the subject. "Did he retire?"

"Technically he hasn't, so I guess I'm still the *acting* chief."

Nick chuckled. "It looked like he'd retired a few years ago, but somebody forgot to mention it to him."

"Nicholas!" my mother exclaimed. "That is not a very nice thing to say!"

"That's okay, Ellen," the captain—acting chief—said. "The old chief was an outstanding police officer in his time, but that time has passed him by. He's gotten a little long in the tooth."

"Long in the tooth? What does that mean?" Nick asked.

"Old," I said.

"How about ancient?" Nick said.

"He's coming up to his seventy-fifth birthday," the acting chief said.

"If he's that old, why doesn't he retire?"

"He will, on his birthday, in two months."

"But he's not really in charge of things now, is he?" Nick asked.

"He remains the chief, but all decisions must be reviewed and approved by me."

"That's good to know," I said. I remembered my one and only experience dealing with the old chief. He'd been yelling and screaming and giving orders that didn't make sense.

"He was a good man, but sometimes age catches up to people." The acting chief paused. "By the way, how old is Mr. McCurdy?"

"He's seventy-four," my mother said.

"But a really young seventy-four," I quickly added. "There's nothing catching up to him. He's fine!"

"Yeah, not only isn't he long in the tooth, he doesn't even *have* many teeth," Nick added.

My mother and the acting chief both laughed.

"He certainly seems pretty quick to me," the acting chief said. "He's an example of somebody who can get older and maintain all his faculties."

"Faculties?" Nick asked.

"Brains…senses…thinking," I explained.

"He's still got all of those for sure," Nick said. "He's one of the best thinkers I know. Heck, he's even smarter than me."

I had the urge to say something, but wisely kept my mouth shut.

"Yes," my mother agreed, "he is a very bright man. It's a shame he never had more formal education." Mr. McCurdy had run away from home when he was kid and joined the circus. He'd become an animal trainer and, when he retired, he came back to the family farm and brought with him some of his circus animals, including Laura, Calvin, Polly, and a couple of others.

"Where's Mr. McCurdy now?" the acting chief asked.

"He's gone for a few days," I answered cautiously, trying to be deliberately vague. There was something about being asked questions by a person in uniform that made this process seem less like a casual conversation.

"He went to get some more animals," Nick said.

So much for being vague. "Not that many," I added, trying to deflect the conversation.

"It's actually a fascinating story," our mother said, beaming.

"Sarah, would you like to tell it to Martin?"

Not really, and I didn't want anybody else to tell him, either. "I'm sure he has more important things to do than listen to me tell some boring story."

He shrugged. "I was off-duty a half hour ago. The only thing on my schedule for the next few hours is dropping your mother off and going home and getting some sleep. I have time."

"It's not that interesting."

"Sarah, don't be so modest. It's a simply *fascinating* story!" Mom said.

"I'll tell him," Nick volunteered.

"No!" I snapped. "I'll do it." The last thing I wanted was for Nick to tell him. Nick was a great storyteller, and I didn't want this story to become more exciting than it already was. We'd kept some of the details from our mother: things like us sneaking into the owners' house; how there had been men who were trying to slaughter the tiger and sell its body parts; and how Nick, me, Vladimir, and Mr. McCurdy had tricked them—actually we'd kept *most* of the story from her.

"Nick and I went away to camp this summer," I began.

"An exotic animal camp," Nick added.

"Interesting," the acting chief said. "I didn't know they had camps like that."

"Neither did we," I said.

"It was a present from their *father*," my mother said coldly. "It's one of his typically inspired ideas." The only thing that impressed her less than my father were his ideas. "The least he could have done was come out east to see them but—"

"Am I going to tell this story or not?" I asked sharply. I was pretty annoyed at my father myself, because it had been over a month since he'd even called us, but that didn't give her the right to pick on him. I was the only one who had that right, and I certainly wasn't going to do it in front of somebody who was practically a stranger.

"Please go on, Sarah," she said.

"Thank you. Anyway, Nick and I were at this camp, and it wasn't very well run, so it was being closed. There was no place for the animals to go, so Mr. McCurdy offered to let them stay here at the farm." What I chose not to say was that Vladimir inherited all the animals after we tricked the old owner—who wanted to sell off the animals—but he had no place to take them until Mr. McCurdy offered his farm.

"Isn't that something?" my mother asked. "Most kids go to camp and come home with a necklace or a T-shirt they made in craft time, but my kids brought back a tiger!"

"Another tiger?" the acting chief asked.

"He's an old tiger," I said.

"But big! Even bigger than Buddha!" Nick said excitedly. "And there's Boo Boo the bear, and the two leopards and—"

"And Vladimir," I said.

"What sort of animal is Vladimir?" the acting chief asked.

Nick and I both started to laugh. "Vladimir's a man," Nick said.

"Really, the animals are Vladimir's, and they'll only be here for a while. He's from Russia and he's a real expert on animals and he's never had any problems with them and he'll be helping Mr. McCurdy and you know that Mr. McCurdy takes good care of his animals and—"

"Sarah," the acting chief said, "just take a deep breath and slow down. It's okay. You don't have anything to worry about."

"That's where you're wrong. Sarah always has to worry about something," Nick said.

"Well, she doesn't have to worry about this. I'm the acting chief of police, not the animal-control officer. I don't care if he has a whole zoo full of animals here at his farm."

"That's great," I said, exhaling.

"I'd be interested in seeing the animals and meeting this Vladimir. He probably has lots of stories to tell."

"Maybe," I said.

"Did you two just get up?" Mom asked.

"No, we've been up for a while," Nick said.

"Then why are you both still in your pajamas?" she asked.

We'd been working so hard and then rushed out so quickly when we heard the car coming that I hadn't even thought about what we were wearing. Thank goodness I hadn't worn my fuzzy, comfy pajamas with the sewn-in feet.

Mom frowned. "And just how did you manage to get your pajamas so dirty?"

I looked down. There were jam and mustard stains on one of my legs.

"What did you have for breakfast?" she asked.

"We didn't have breakfast yet, but we fed Laura, Polly, and Calvin already," Nick said.

"It's encouraging to hear you're taking good care of the animals, but what about the two of you?" she asked.

"We can't eat until we feed Buddha. He still needs breakfast."

"Buddha, the tiger?" the acting chief asked.

"Yeah."

"Do you think I could come and watch?" he asked.

"Sure…I guess that's okay."

"That is, if your mother has time." He turned to Mom. "Would it be all right if I got you to town a little bit later?"

"I'm just a passenger. Besides, it would be reassuring to have you here while they feed Buddha. Unlike my children, I'm still nervous around that tiger."

I gave a weak little smile. What my mother didn't know was that Buddha still made me a lot more than just a little nervous. They followed us back into the farmhouse as Nick and I went to get changed out of our pajamas.

"Is that monkey in here somewhere?" the acting chief asked.

"Calvin's not a monkey. He's a chimp. He's here," I called back over my shoulder.

"He's probably sleeping," Nick added. "He was up pretty

early this morning and probably went back to bed."

"It's nice to know somebody had an early morning," our mother said.

I ignored what she said and looked around the kitchen. Laura was asleep on the couch, while neither Calvin nor Polly were to be seen.

"The kitchen is spotless!" my mother exclaimed. "I've never seen it look this good."

"Thanks. I'm trying to get the place in good shape before Mr. McCurdy gets back."

"You're off to a good start." My mother glanced at her watch. I knew she was supposed to be at work already, preparing for an upcoming trial.

"I'll get changed quickly," I said. I went to my bedroom, closing the door behind me. My clothes were neatly arranged on the chair beside my bed. I started to change. Despite everything the acting chief had said, I was uncomfortable having him around and wanted to get both him and my mother out of here as soon as possible. I balled up my pajamas and tossed them into the corner. I'd take care of things later.

Coming back into the kitchen, I found the acting chief standing beside Laura. She was still sleeping on the couch. Carefully, slowly, he reached down and touched her side, giving her a little pat. Laura didn't move.

"Let's go to the barn and feed Buddha, so you can get on your way," I said.

Nick came down the hall, still buttoning his shirt.

"Let's go," I said.

We left the house and went down the little lane to the barn. It was a big old run-down building with missing and weathered boards, and the roof had holes that let in the rain. We went down the side so we could enter the stable. Unlike the main floor, the stable was warm and snug and dry.

I flicked on the switch, and the fluorescent lights started to hum and then came to life, illuminating the stable. There were bales of hay stacked up to the ceiling along the far wall, and a large pile of straw occupied the centre of the stable. Along the walls there were stalls—empty cattle stalls with old, rusty bars—that extended halfway up to the ceiling. The only one that was different was at the far end of the barn. In that double stall, specially fitted so the bars reached the ceiling, sat Buddha—Mr. McCurdy's fully grown, eight-hundred-pound Siberian tiger. He was lying down at the back corner of his pen, curled in a ball like a big kitty.

As we walked toward him, Buddha got up, stretched, and started moving toward the front of his pen. There was something about seeing him walking toward me that was exciting and thrilling and scary all at once. It always made me take a deep breath. In my head I knew that Buddha was tame—at least semi-tame—and was safely behind the bars. But often my head didn't communicate well with my stomach. It did a little flip at the sight of the tiger.

"Wow," the acting chief said under his breath.

"It's an amazing sight, isn't it?" my mother added. "At least for us. For Sarah and Nick, I guess it gets almost boring because they see it so often."

"Nothing special," Nick said, agreeing with her.

I didn't agree, but didn't say anything. I thought that I could walk in here every day for a thousand years and still have it affect my stomach the same way.

Buddha pressed against the bars and began to rub his head back and forth. Nick reached through the bars and stroked Buddha behind the ear.

"Nicholas, should you be doing that?" our mother asked anxiously.

"He likes it. Do you want to give him a little head scratch?"

"No! Of course not." She stopped. "You were joking...right?"

"I was joking, but you could scratch him if you wanted to."

Mom held up her hands and vigorously shook her head.

"Could I?" the acting chief asked. "Could I give him a little pat?"

"Sure," Nick said. "Come over here."

The acting chief hesitated for a split second, as if he suddenly thought better of what he'd requested, then shuffled forward until he stood right beside Nick in front of Buddha.

"Just reach through the bars and rub him right here," Nick said.

Tentatively the acting chief reached in and placed his hand on Buddha's head and rubbed. "He's so soft."

"Especially that spot," Nick agreed. "Is this the first time you've touched a tiger?"

"That's for sure."

"Sure you don't want to pet him, too, Mom?" Nick asked.

"I'm sure. The only thing I'd rather do less than pet the tiger is snuggle with that snake," she said.

"Brent is a very snuggleable python," Nick said. "Soft and warm."

"I'm sure he is," she said, "and I bet he wouldn't harm a kitten."

Nick and I exchanged a look. "Actually he would harm a kitten," Nick said. "Or a cat or a small dog or—"

"But not a person," I said, trying to soften what Nick was saying. "He isn't nearly big enough to harm a person."

"Not big enough!" our mother exclaimed. "I've seen him, and he must be over four metres long."

"He's not that big. Three metres tops," I said.

"Oh, good. That makes it so much better." She paused. "That snake lives out here in the barn, doesn't it?"

"First off, *it* is a *he*, and yes, Brent does live out here," I replied.

"And it—he—doesn't have a pen? He's free to just wander around the entire barn…is that correct?" she asked as she gazed nervously around the barn.

"That's right, but you don't have to worry. He spends most of his time under that pile of straw in the centre," I said, pointing behind where my mother stood.

She turned to face the pile and took a few steps back.

"When he's not in the straw, he's most likely to be in the—" I stopped as I looked up and saw Brent wrapped around the beam, no more than a half metre above my mother's head!

"He likes to be where?" my mother questioned anxiously.

For a split second I couldn't even choke out a word. "What?" I finally sputtered.

"You were saying that when he wasn't in the straw he was someplace else, but you didn't finish your sentence. Where is he the rest of the time?"

I had been about to say hanging from the beams. "Um…if he isn't in the straw…he's…he's way over there in those bales of hay against the far wall."

My mother let out a big sigh. "That's good to know. I'll just stay away from both those places."

"I knew about the straw, but I didn't think he liked those bales," Nick said. "I thought that he spent the rest of his time hanging—"

"Around those bales on the far wall!" I snapped, cutting Nick off. I motioned upward with my eyes, and Nick looked up and saw Brent. His eyes widened and his mouth dropped wide open.

"Is something wrong, Nicholas?" our mother asked. She was staring at him.

He shook his head. That stunned look was still plastered on his face. As we stood there, Brent began to slowly lower his head toward Mom. Suddenly I remembered why Brent liked being in the beams. In the wild Burmese pythons climbed into low-lying trees, and the beams reminded him of those trees. There they waited until something passed underneath and then they dropped onto their prey and—oh, goodness, was he going to do that to my mother?

"Mom!" I screamed as I grabbed her and practically yanked her off her feet.

"Sarah, what's gotten into you?" she demanded, her expression reflecting the look of shock on Nick's face, but for a very different reason.

"Nothing...nothing at all...I just wanted you to help get Buddha his food!"

"Fine, I'll help you get him his food, but there's no need to get so excited." If she had looked up, the word *excited* would have taken on a whole new meaning.

"It's just I know you have to get to work, and I didn't want to waste any more of your time. Nick, could you take Mom with you to fill up the feed bucket?"

"Sure, sure, no problem...right away," he said, grasping Mom's hand and leading her away.

"It's certainly nice to see you two being this cooperative with each other," Mom said, looking back over her shoulder as Nick dragged her to the freezer that held Buddha's food.

"Is your mother afraid of snakes?" the acting chief asked quietly.

"I guess she's a little nervous," I said.

"Just a little?" he asked. "Because that snake up there coiled around the beams could scare the living daylights out of most people."

I didn't know what to say.

"It was smart of you to get her away without letting her know where it was." He paused. "But you've always been pretty quick on your feet, haven't you?"

I looked at the ground. I knew exactly what he was referring to. Mr. McCurdy, Nick, and I had once tricked the whole police department. Buddha had escaped and we had gotten him back, safe and sound, by pretending we were animal experts who'd been called in by the chief—the old chief.

"But your mother is going to be back here in a little while and that snake doesn't look like it's going anywhere."

"I'll take care of that." I reached over and grabbed a broom that was leaning against a post. Turning it around so I was holding it by the bristles, I raised it and gently poked Brent in some of his many ribs. He didn't move. I pressed harder and he started to squirm. I nudged him again and he began to climb higher into the rafters, away from my prodding. Slowly he moved out of reach. His middle followed his head, which was followed by his tail, and he disappeared into the darkness. Out of sight and out of mind.

"I think you'll have to hold that broom a little differently if you're planning on cleaning up," Nick said as he and Mom returned.

"It seemed to work pretty well this way," I said as I flipped it back around and leaned it against the post. "You got the food?"

"Two chickens," he said, holding up the bucket to show me.

"Does he always eat that much?" my mother asked.

"Sometimes he has different things, but he generally eats the equivalent of four chickens every day," I said.

"That's a lot of chicken. Fourteen hundred chickens in a year!" she said. "That's a lot of money for Mr. McCurdy."

I hadn't really thought about that. Two tigers would mean twice as many chickens, not to mention what the lions and leopards and bear would eat. This was going to cost a lot of money. Where was Mr. McCurdy going to get that sort of—

"That was a strange sound," the acting chief said.

"What sound?" Nick asked.

"It was like Buddha had just sprung a leak and air was escaping."

"Oh, you mean the puffing. That's a good sound. That's the sound a tiger makes when it's happy to see you."

"Or happy to see the feed bucket," I added.

"Or both," Nick said. "Do you want to hear the sound a tiger makes when he's not happy to see you?"

"Sure," the acting chief said.

"Listen carefully." Nick crouched slightly down and everybody listened. He didn't make a sound. Then Nick burst into a grin. "Actually a tiger doesn't make any sound when he's not happy to see you—he just kills you." That was an old joke of Mr. McCurdy's.

"Nicholas!" my mother scolded him.

"Since you don't want to pet him, do you want to feed Buddha?" Nick asked our mother.

"I think I'll pass on that, too."

"Chief?" Nick asked.

"I'll just watch."

Nick reached into the bucket and pulled out a chicken. It still had its head and feet and wings and feathers. As he strolled down the side of the pen, Buddha watched him intensely, following him with his eyes.

"You want a chicken, Buddha, old buddy boy?" Nick asked as he pushed the chicken through the bars and dropped it.

In answer Buddha pounced, covering the four metres between him and Nick in one leap. Catching the chicken, Buddha grabbed it with his teeth. There was a sickening crunch as his powerful jaws crushed the bones of the bird. I shuddered involuntarily. While Buddha's attention was on the one chicken, I took the second bird out of the bucket and tossed it between the bars and into his pen.

"How long will it take him to finish breakfast?" my mother asked.

"The eating part could be just a couple of minutes," I said, "but first he'll want to prepare his meal."

"What does that mean?"

"Buddha doesn't like the feathers. Mr. McCurdy says they tickle on the way down, so Buddha plucks the chicken before he eats it."

Buddha was already at work. Holding the bird between his two front paws, he was pulling out feathers with his teeth and dropping them to the side.

"At camp we used to pluck them for the cats," I said.

"And chop off their feet and heads," Nick added.

Our mother shuddered.

"It's okay, Mom," Nick said. "They were already dead."

"Feeding time's over," I said. "You two better get going."

"Sarah, if I didn't know you better, I'd swear you were trying to get rid of us," Mom said.

"Of course I'm not trying to get rid of you," I answered. "It's just I know you have lots of work to do, and if you don't finish it now you'll have to finish it tonight, and then you can't join us for dinner…that's all."

"That's very sweet." She came over and gave me a little kiss on the cheek and a hug. She did the same to Nick. "I'll see you two later tonight. Be good, and be safe."

The acting chief nodded goodbye and the two of them left the stable. I breathed a sigh of relief. "Would you do me a favour?" I asked Nick.

"Depends. Is it easy?"

"It's simple. The next time you start to talk about us going away to camp and the things that happened—don't. Just keep your mouth shut."

"Come on, Sarah, I didn't say anything I shouldn't have."

"You were close. There's lots of things it's better Mom doesn't know, and even worse…don't talk around that guy."

"Why not? He's seems like a pretty good guy."

"Just don't! Okay?"

Nick shrugged. "Sure. It's not like I'm going to be running into him every day or anything."

"Thank you. Now let's go back inside and I'll make us both some breakfast."

"Now you're talking, Sarah." We left the barn and started toward the house when I heard the sound of somebody driving up the lane.

"Do you think they forgot something?" Nick asked.

"I don't know. I just wish they'd both go away and—"

I stopped mid-sentence. Slowly driving up the lane was a gigantic tractor trailer truck.

Chapter 3

Nick and I stared as the gigantic truck came to a stop with a loud huffing of its air brakes.

"Who is that and what does he—"

Mr. McCurdy popped his head out of the driver's side window of the rig! He had on a baseball cap, his grey hair sticking out from under it in a thousand different directions. He was wearing his special driving glasses—special because they helped him see, but also because they were pink women's cat's-eye glasses, covered in rhinestones, he'd bought at a flea market.

"Sarah! Nick!" he yelled, waving to us.

Running to the side of the truck, we looked up—way up—to where he sat. He opened the door and started to climb down. He looked so small against the massive truck. I was afraid he might fall, so I tried to get underneath him and catch him if he did.

"What are you doing here?" I asked.

"I live here, remember?"

"Of course, but—"

"I just asked you to watch my house for a few days, not move in for good!"

"I...I mean, I just wasn't expecting you back at least until tomorrow, or even a couple of days from now."

"By the time I got there, Vladimir had already gotten a lot of the work done. There wasn't much left for me to do but load the animals in the trucks."

"Trucks? As in more than one?" Nick asked.

"Like one plus one. Vladimir is driving the second. He should be here soon."

"But where did you get these trucks from?" I asked.

"I called in a couple of favours. I still know a lot of people in the circus business, so I borrowed a couple of rigs."

I looked at the side of the truck. In big, bold letters it said BICKFORD BROTHERS CIRCUS. Underneath the words was a gigantic picture of a tiger jumping through a flaming hoop.

"Do you think Buddha could do that?" Nick asked, gesturing to the picture.

"Look a little closer at that there picture," Mr. McCurdy said.

"Is that…is that Buddha?" I stammered.

"Can't you tell?" he asked. "That was in his younger days."

"But I thought the circus you worked for went out of business," I said.

"It did, so they sold off the equipment, including this truck. The Bickford Brothers left the picture but painted out the name of that circus and added their name."

Nick stared up at the graphic. "Wow, that's amazing! I didn't know Buddha could do tricks like that."

"He can do all sorts of things. Buddha is one smart tiger, and I was one smart trainer. Sounds like you were doubting one of us was smart."

Nick smiled. He always was able to figure out faster than I could when Mr. McCurdy was joking around. "I never had any doubts about the *tiger*."

Mr. McCurdy chuckled. "Did I travel all this way to get this sort of grief?"

"Could Buddha still do tricks like that?" Nick asked.

"He could, but he ain't going to ever again."

"Why not?" Nick asked. "It would be cool."

"No, it wouldn't," Mr. McCurdy said. "What it would be is *hot*…very hot. And dangerous. How'd you like it if I made you jump through a ring of fire?"

"You wouldn't have to *make* me," Nick said. "Build me a ramp and I'll get on my roller blades. I'll jump through all by myself."

I shook my head. I knew he wasn't joking, and that was the scary part. Put my brother on his aggressive in-line skates, and he'd jump and grind and spin until he either got really tired, or fell down and hurt himself. It seemed to end either way about the same number of times.

"Maybe you'd do it gladly, but a smart animal like Buddha wouldn't want to go anywhere near fire. All animals are afraid of fire." Mr. McCurdy paused. "Hated to train animals to do things like that."

"Then why did you?" Nick asked.

"Not much choice. I didn't own the circus. I just worked there. 'Sides, the crowds loved it when something looked flashy, and nothing's as flashy as fire."

"But Buddha would still know how to do it, wouldn't he?" Nick persisted.

"We're not going to find out. Buddha and me are retired. Nobody's ever going to make either of us jump through any hoops ever again."

"They made *you* jump through flaming hoops?" Nick asked in amazement, and Mr. McCurdy burst into laughter.

"Nick, it's just an expression." I explained.

"It wasn't with Buddha," Nick argued.

"But it is with people. It means making people do things they don't want to."

"That's right," Mr. McCurdy agreed. "And now that I'm an old man, I've earned the right not to have to do anything that I don't want to. Buddha's earned the same right."

"Where's your car?" I asked. Mr. McCurdy drove an old pink convertible.

"I lent it to the same guy I borrowed the trucks from. They don't need the trucks for a week 'cause they're set up in town, so he'll drive around in my car until he needs to load up and move to the next place."

Suddenly the sound of another truck could be heard. I turned and saw a second big rig creeping along the rutted driveway. It pulled up and halted right behind the first. The truck had barely stopped moving when the driver's door burst open and out came Vladimir. The second truck was the same size as the first, but it seemed smaller compared to Vladimir. He was just about the biggest human being I'd ever seen, and somehow he looked even bigger than I remembered. Leaping to the ground, he came charging toward us, and I felt myself fight to take a step back. I knew Vladimir was just a big, friendly teddy bear, but with his massive size, his beard, and his long hair, he reminded me of a grizzly bear.

"Vladimir!" Nick called out as he rushed to meet him.

"Nicoli!" he screamed. Vladimir wrapped his arms around my brother, and Nick practically disappeared from view as the Russian picked him off the ground and spun him around. He then gave Nick a big kiss on first one cheek and then the other!

"So good to see Nicky!" he said with his thick accent as he put my brother back on the ground. "And big girl Sarah!" he bellowed. "Good to see!" He reached out and grabbed me, practically pulling me off my feet. Wrapping me in his arms, he *did* pull me off the ground. Vladimir spun me around, and I felt like a little rag doll. He gave me a kiss on both cheeks, as well, before returning me to the ground.

"Don't you even think about picking me up, you big lug!" Mr. McCurdy warned. "I want my spine to stay in one piece! You understand?"

Vladimir nodded. "*Da, da*, understand." Walking over, he gave Mr. McCurdy a kiss on one cheek and tried to plant one on the other side before Mr. McCurdy pulled away.

"Now, you just go stopping that, as well!" Mr. McCurdy yelled as he wiped his cheek with the back of an old, wrinkled hand.

"But Vladimir always kiss cheeks of friends. Angus not friend?" he asked, sounding hurt.

"Of course I'm your friend! It's just that men don't go around kissing each other!"

"In Russia men kiss friends."

"This ain't Russia. Here we just shake hands or give a little slap on the back—but then again, with those paws of yours it might be better if you don't go around slapping people, in case they go flying across the room. Understand?"

"*Da*, Vladimir understand."

"Good, because we don't have no time for me to be teaching you about manners. Not when we've got all these animals to unload."

The animals! In all the excitement of the trucks arriving, I'd forgotten what was in them.

"Let's see how they all did on the trip," Mr. McCurdy said.

Vladimir and Mr. McCurdy circled around to the back of the first truck. Nick and I followed so closely that we almost tripped on their heels. Vladimir reached up and flipped a big bolt, slid it to the side, and the big door swung open.

"Let's go in and have a look," Mr. McCurdy said. He put a foot on the bumper and started to climb into the trailer. He was part-way up when he seemed to waver. I gasped. Was he going to fall? I started to run over to catch him when I was bumped out of the way by Vladimir. He'd moved as fast as a cat to get beneath Mr. McCurdy, his hands ready to catch him. Mr. McCurdy grabbed the handle and regained his balance, pulling himself up. Vladimir quickly put down his hands. I knew, and I guessed Vladimir did, as well, that Mr. McCurdy wouldn't have been happy with us trying to "save" him.

"Want help up?" Vladimir asked.

"Not me," Nick answered. He scrambled into the back of the trailer.

"Big girl, Sarah?" he asked.

It looked pretty high. A little help wouldn't hurt anybody. "Sure...thanks."

Vladimir took my hand, and as I went to put a foot on the bumper, I felt myself being lifted and placed in the back of the trailer. I'd expected a hand, not an elevator ride! Vladimir climbed in beside me.

"This is amazing!" Nick yelled.

I turned. For once he wasn't just exaggerating. The entire truck was filled with animals. There was an aisle down the middle, and both sides were lined with cages. In each one there was an animal. The first cage held the big male lion, Simba. He was lying on his side, eyes closed. Beside him were his mate and two little cubs. The mother was also lying down, and the cubs were nursing. On the other side of the aisle, in the same pen, were the two leopards. They were curled together in a little ball in the back corner. They looked content to be there, as if to say, "As long as we're together, we're happy."

Beside them was Boo Boo, the black bear. As Mr. McCurdy and Vladimir walked by, she made a sound like a bawling baby and put both paws against the bars.

"How my baby bear?" Vladimir asked as he bent and pressed his face close. Boo Boo pushed her face against the cage. Her tongue snaked between the bars and licked Vladimir's face. I shuddered. Boo Boo had just about the worst breath in the entire world.

I walked past Vladimir and stopped in front of the pens holding the two jaguars. They were glaring at me, and the tips of both of their tails were waving back and forth. They weren't happy— probably about the truck ride, or being in the small cage, or me being here. I knew enough about jaguars to know they were probably the most unpredictable, dangerous, and least trainable of all the cats. I knew all of that without any real experience. I was going to try to keep it that way.

There was a puffing noise, and I turned around. There was Kushna, Vladimir's big old Siberian tiger. He puffed again. I was glad he was happy to see me. I knew it was crazy, but I thought he understood I'd been part of saving him from those poachers. In my head I figured that it was just wishful thinking, but somehow I thought he sensed it.

Mr. McCurdy stooped beside Kushna's pen. The tiger came forward and rubbed his head back and forth the way Buddha had a few minutes earlier. Mr. McCurdy reached in and began scratching the old cat behind the ears. I had the urge to ask if I could do the same, but this wasn't the time or place.

"Start unloading now, boss?" Vladimir asked.

"Not yet. First let's check the other truck."

"Are my girls in the other truck?" I asked anxiously.

"Course they are. What did you think we'd do, sell 'em?" Mr. McCurdy asked.

"We go see all other animals." Vladimir turned to Mr. McCurdy. "Unless Angus want Vladimir to give food and water to Boo Boo and cats first?"

"They can wait a few minutes more. 'Sides, I wanna have your help with the other animals. Let's go."

I walked carefully down the very middle of the aisle between the cages, trying to keep equal distance from the animals on both sides. Vladimir jumped from the truck, and Nick followed closely behind. The Russian reached up and offered me a hand. Cautiously I took it, and he helped me down. I'd been afraid he was going to pick me up again. Mr. McCurdy came next, and Vladimir moved slightly away, not offering a hand. Instead, as Mr. McCurdy turned to climb down, Vladimir moved back, standing right behind him, ready to catch him if he fell. As he got close to the bottom, Vladimir darted out of the way so Mr. McCurdy wouldn't notice him.

Nick rushed off to the second truck, with Vladimir following almost as quickly. I stayed behind, walking with Mr. McCurdy. He was moving very slowly—more than usual—and looked tired. I wondered how much he'd slept over the past three days, how much he'd had to eat. I knew the last thing on his mind would have been taking care of himself.

"Don't worry, Sarah. I'm sure they remember you," Mr. McCurdy said.

"What?"

"The girls. I'm sure they remember you. Isn't that what you're worried about? You sure do look worried."

What was I supposed to say—that I was worried about him? He wouldn't appreciate that any more than he would Vladimir standing by to catch him. Mr. McCurdy was one stubborn, proud old bird.

"Yeah...that's what I'm worried about," I lied.

"Thought so," he cackled. "I know you so well. I can read you like a book."

By the time we'd reached the back of the truck, the door was already open and Nick and Vladimir were in the back of the trailer.

"How are they?" Mr. McCurdy called up. "Any fatalities?"

"Fatalities? You mean deaths?" I gasped. "Some of the animals are dead?" My girls were just little—they'd be the most vulnerable!

"Hot, tired, but good. Sure good. Come see," Vladimir said.

I scrambled up the side of the truck like a mountain goat. I wanted to see the girls. I wanted to see all the animals. Immediately I was struck by a major difference. There was a terrible odour in this trailer.

"It stinks in here!" Nick said, voicing my thoughts. "Smells like something died!"

Oh, my gosh...was he right?

"It's just the smell of so many animals is such a small space," Mr. McCurdy said. "Don't go worrying your sister any more than you have to."

Of course, there were more animals. The whole place was filled with animals. There were the three giant buffalo in stalls at the side, more than a dozen deer, and Peanuts the elephant.

"There are your babies," Mr. McCurdy said.

One whole side of the trailer was home to the deer. There were legs and spotted bodies and antlers all jammed together. And there, right at the front, side by side, stood my little girls. I bent by the bars and reached in.

"Come here, girls." They didn't move. "It's me...it's your mommy."

Of course, I wasn't really their mother, but I had been there when they were born. Vladimir had had to deliver one of them, because their mother was having trouble. He was able to help the second of the twins, but the mother hadn't lived. That was one of the saddest things that had ever happened to me in my whole life. Because their mother was dead, we had to wash and feed them. Since it was me who did most of it, the two little deer had decided I was their mother.

As I watched, one of them walked up to another deer and began suckling! The second one quickly joined the first.

"They have new mommy to feed," Vladimir said.

"That's great," I said. "I guess that means they don't need me. Although I hoped they'd at least remember me and—" I stopped as a soft little mouth started to suckle on one of my fingers. Then a second deer grabbed another finger.

"Nobody ever forgets their mamma," Mr. McCurdy said.

"Can we take them out?" I asked. "Can we?"

"They'll be among the very first animals we take out. But first we have to give 'em all some food and water, and then let 'em calm down after the trip."

"Plan good," Vladimir said. "After animals fed, give water, they more easy to handle. Then we move into new pens."

"Well, we have one more step to do before that," Mr. McCurdy told him.

Vladimir gave him a questioning look.

"We still have to *build* the pens."

Chapter 4

I walked slowly up the wooden ramp to the back of the trailer. It slumped slightly under the combined weight of me and the two buckets of water I was carrying. The buckets were full to the brim, and they kept bumping into my legs, spilling water over the edge. The lower part of my pants and my high-top basketball shoes were soaked. With each step my feet squished.

As soon as I entered the trailer, every eye was on me. The animals surged forward, coming closer to the bars of the pens. This was my twenty-third trip, and each time I'd returned with my full buckets, the water I'd brought on the previous trip had already vanished. I was amazed at how much water they could suck down. Then again, it was a hot day inside a metal trailer and there were a whole lot of rather big animals in here. I was hot, and I was just wearing shorts and a T-shirt. Each of them was wearing a fur coat. Thank goodness Vladimir had moved the trucks into the shade so the sun wasn't beating directly on them anymore.

I put one bucket down, and with both hands emptied the second into the trough in the deer's pen. They all pushed and jostled and bumped one another to get at the water. My poor little babies scrambled underneath everybody else's feet. Even their adopted mother didn't seem to be giving them any special care.

"Be careful!" I yelled. "They're just babies!"

They ignored me. The little ones seemed to be doing okay, though. The deer, Samantha and Sarah, both managed to get their noses into the water. They were getting bigger and more able to care for themselves. Although, even when they were fully grown and even bigger than I was, I'd still be worried about them. My mother told me that was what parenthood was all about.

I reached for the other bucket. It was gone! How could a bucket just disappear? It must be somewhere or—"Peanuts!" I yelled. The bucket was beside the elephant's pen, and he was drinking the water. He must have reached out and pulled the bucket close enough so he could drink. I grabbed for the bucket. It was completely empty. Boy, could elephants drink!

"Obviously you're all still thirsty," I said to the animals.

Vladimir had told me I was to keep getting water until the trough was full and they turned their noses up when I offered them more. That looked as if it was going to be a long time— maybe forever.

"Aren't you finished yet?" Nick asked as I left the trailer and started back down the ramp.

"Not even close."

Nick smirked. "I guess one of us made a better choice than the other."

We had decided we'd each take care of the animals in one of the trucks. All the big cats and Boo Boo had made me nervous, so I'd chosen to water and feed the ones that didn't consider me a source of food. Maybe that had been the safer choice, but it certainly hadn't been the easier one.

"You could help," I said, trying to hand him a bucket.

He refused to take it from me. "I *could* help, but I don't think I will. You didn't offer to help me."

"That's because there was almost nothing to your job!"

"I had to do things," he protested. "I gave each cat a chicken, and I had to go all the way down to the barn to get them."

"Big deal! I had to get water for all my animals!"

"I had to get water for the animals in my trailer, too!"

"Ha! I bet it only took you five or six trips!"

"About that," he admitted.

"I've already made over *thirty* trips!" I said, exaggerating to make it seem even worse than it was.

"A deal's a deal."

"Come on, Nick."

"I guess one of us just chose smarter," Nick said, "or maybe one of us was just too big a chicken to be around the animals with sharp teeth."

He had me there, but I didn't want him to know it. "I have no idea what you're talking about. The animals in my trailer are just as dangerous as the ones in yours."

"Are you joking?" Nick scoffed.

"No, I'm not. I'll put my animals up against yours any day of the week!"

"Yeah, right, a deer against a tiger. That'd be a great contest!" he snapped.

"Not as good as an elephant against a tiger! No contest there, either! Forget the mangy tigers or lions, because I've got the *real* king of the jungle in my trailer!"

I suddenly got an idea. I knew how much Nick had enjoyed riding Peanuts while we were away at camp.

"I've got the only animal you can ride!" I said with a smirk. "Every time I bring up more water or some hay for Peanuts, who do you think he's getting to like more? It certainly won't be you! There's an old saying: 'An elephant never forgets.' Peanuts will remember that I was the one bringing him stuff—"

"Can I help?" Nick pleaded.

"No way. A deal's a deal. I'm going to take care of Peanuts. After all, if I have to do all the work with the other animals, there's no way I'm going to let you take care of the elephant!"

"How about if I help with all the animals?" Nick asked.

"The deer and buffalo, too?" I asked.

He nodded.

I didn't answer right away. I wanted him to believe I was really thinking it over. What I was thinking was what an idiot he was. "Okay. You got yourself a new deal. Here, take the buckets."

Nick took them from me, and I turned and began to walk away so he wouldn't see the grin on my face.

"Hey!" Nick called out. I turned around, wiping my face clean. "Where are you going?"

"Me? I'm going to get more hay for the animals. I'll be back in a while." I walked up the lane toward the house and barn. The only hay I wanted was a big bale to lie down and go to sleep on. None of the last three nights I'd slept at Mr. McCurdy's had been good sleep, but last night was terrible. Combined with all the work we'd done today, both in the kitchen and now with the animals, I thought I could fall asleep standing up.

Just off to the side of the lane, Vladimir and Mr. McCurdy were working. Vladimir had been driving poles into the ground, and Mr. McCurdy was hammering fencing that had been placed against the poles. They were creating a temporary pen for the deer and buffalo. A square about twenty metres on all sides, it was going to be a lot smaller than the pen they'd had back at the animal camp, but would certainly be bigger than the truck. Besides, it was just going to be for a while until they could build something larger.

I was amazed at how fast they were working. They'd already put up three sides and were starting on the fourth. Vladimir was like a machine. I got the feeling he really didn't need that big sledgehammer—he could have used his hands to drive the poles into the ground.

The place they'd selected was partially shaded by trees. I noticed they'd strung the fence out so that some of the trees formed posts. That was smart in more ways than one. They didn't have to drive in as many poles, and it also gave the animals some shade. I wiped my brow with the back of my hand. It was awfully hot in the full summer sun. I wondered how Mr. McCurdy was doing. I changed directions and headed toward them.

Mr. McCurdy was crouched down, holding one of the poles while Vladimir hammered it into the ground. There hadn't been much rain this summer, and I knew the ground must be pretty hard. Each time Vladimir raised the gigantic hammer over his head, ready to swing, I cringed. If he ever missed, he'd drive Mr. McCurdy into the ground. I came up quietly from behind and watched silently as they finished. Mr. McCurdy slowly got to his feet. He looked tired.

"How's it going, Sarah?"

"Good. One trailer's completely fed and watered, and Nick and I are more than halfway finished the second one." I paused. "How's it going for you two?"

"Much work. Much to do," Vladimir said. "But finished nearly on this pen. What you think?"

"It looks good. Do you want something to drink? Or maybe a lunch break?" I asked.

"Water might be good, but there's no time to eat until the animals are taken care of," Mr. McCurdy said.

"But wouldn't it be better if we took a short break?" I asked.

"They'll be plenty of time for resting tonight," he said. "You tired, Sarah?"

I *was* tired, but it wasn't me who I thought should take a break. "A little. I just thought that it would be best for all of us to eat and then—"

"Couldn't rest till I know those animals are doing better. The cats and the bear are okay for a while, but the others—the deer and buffalo especially—need to get out. They're too cramped and crowded. Can you really take a break knowing those little deer of yours aren't doing well?" he asked.

"No, I guess not," I admitted. "Is there anything I can do here to make things happen faster?"

"I don't see you being much use driving poles or stringing fence, but there is one thing that could help."

"What's that?"

"Go back to the house and get every last piece of my clothes. Everything."

"Your clothes?" I asked in confusion.

"Yeah. Every single sock and shirt and pair of underwear. Understand?"

I shrugged. "I guess so."

"And you know the clothesline out the back of the house?"

"You want me to wash your clothes?" I asked in disbelief.

"Not wash 'em. Bring 'em here. And the clothesline. Cut it down and bring it to me."

This was making less and less sense to me by the second. Maybe I should have kept my mouth shut and continued to give the animals water.

"So, you going to do it, or just stand there staring at me?" Mr. McCurdy asked.

"Um...sure."

I stumbled toward the house. I had no idea whatsoever what he had in mind, but I knew whatever it was, it would work.

Mr. McCurdy and Vladimir were finishing up the last side of the temporary pen. I'd been instructed to cut the clothesline into two pieces. I'd strung them both up, one line attached to the side of the trailer door and leading all the way—about twenty-five metres—to the small opening they'd left in the pen. The second line was hung from the other side of the trailer door to the other side of the fence opening so that the two lines created a corridor from the trailer to the pen. I finished pinning up the last of Mr. McCurdy's clothes to one of the lines. The two lines contained every piece of clothing he owned. There were socks, shirts, pants, underwear, sweaters, and long johns all fluttering in the wind.

As I'd been working, Mr. McCurdy had told me what was going to happen. The lines were supposed to guide the animals toward the pen, and the clothes waving in the wind were to scare them and keep them away from the lines and moving forward. It certainly sounded like an interesting theory. We'd soon see if it worked.

"Well, Sarah, you all done?" Mr. McCurdy asked.

"That's everything you own," I said. "Do you think this is going to work?"

"Sure. Positive. No problem," he said.

"You've done this before…right?" I asked.

"Not technically."

"What does that mean?"

"It means I've never actually done it before, but I've thought about it. Let's find out if I'm right."

"And if you're not?" I asked.

"Then we're going to have to figure out how to round up a bunch of deer and buffalo," Mr. McCurdy said.

"How do we do that?" I questioned.

"I'm not really sure, but I'm not worried."

"You're not?"

He shook his head. "I'm sure you'll come up with something."

"Me? You expect me to—"

He cackled with laughter. "Sarah, you worry way too much for somebody so young. It'll work. You'll see."

I walked beside Mr. McCurdy toward the trailer. Nick and Vladimir were already waiting for us.

"So how we do this, boss?" Vladimir asked.

"You and me go into the trailer. We open up the enclosures and let the animals out one at a time."

"What do we do?" Nick asked.

"You and Sarah stay out of the trailer," Mr. McCurdy said.

That was good. It could be pretty dangerous to be inside a trailer with an angry buffalo or three.

"I need you to each take a different side of the line and try to keep 'em moving," Mr. McCurdy told them.

"How do we do that?" Nick asked.

"Yell at 'em, wave your arms in the air."

I figured I could do that.

"One more thing," Mr. McCurdy said. "If any of the animals tries to break through the line, you just stop 'em."

"Stop them?" I gasped.

He nodded.

"You want me to try to stop a runaway buffalo?"

"Just remember, they're more afraid of you than you are of them."

If he was right, they must be downright terrified.

❖

Nick and I stood on opposite sides of the two lines filled with flapping clothes. Between us was a corridor about five metres wide. We were no more than a dozen metres from the ramp leading down from the trailer. Mr. McCurdy and Vladimir were both inside the trailer. Vladimir was going to work the gate to the pens while Mr. McCurdy would shoo the animals through the door and down the ramp. Once they left the ramp, Nick and I would chase them until they were inside the pen. That was how it was supposed to work. We'd soon find out

"*Yeehaa!*" Mr. McCurdy screamed, his voice echoing from inside the trailer.

I turned in time to see a deer—a big buck with antlers—appear at the top of the ramp. His eyes were wide, and he looked scared and confused. I knew exactly how he must be feeling.

"*Get moving!*" Mr. McCurdy yelled as he reached out and smacked the deer in the rump with his hat. The deer jumped down the length of the ramp, landed on the grass, and galloped at a full run. Before I could even think to react, he was past me. Charging down the corridor formed by the two lines, he covered the twenty-five metres in seconds and entered the pen. The deer raced around the perimeter of the pen and started to slow down. Coming to a stop in the very centre, he glanced around, put his head down, and began to graze!

"That didn't seem too hard," Nick said.

"Maybe they'll all be that easy," I said.

"I hope not."

"You hope not?" I asked in amazement.

"Don't you want a little more challenge in your life?"

"No! I just want things to go according to plan!"

"That's *boring*…but then again…so are you," Nick said.

"I may be boring, but at least I'm not a—"

"Get moving!" Mr. McCurdy yelled, and we turned to see another deer—no, two deer—at the top of the ramp. They bounded down the ramp and skidded to a halt on the grass.

Nick waved his hat above his head and yelled. The deer jumped into the air and dashed down the corridor. They entered the pen quickly and joined the big buck in the middle of the field. Again, exactly what we'd hoped for. There wasn't much time to celebrate, though, because another deer was already coming down the ramp. It ran along the corridor in a dozen strides, hitting the pen and stopping among the others that were already grazing.

Deer were such herd animals that this should have gotten easier with each one. They'd each want to run to the increasingly large cluster of deer already waiting in the pen so they could rejoin the herd.

Two more deer thundered past me toward the pen, then another, and another, and another. I looked back at the trailer and saw more deer getting ready to come down—and there were Sarah and Samantha! The rest of the deer all wanted to join up with the herd. They trotted past us toward the pen, with Sarah and Samantha running along behind the last of the big deer.

"Way to go, girls!" I yelled at them, and they both slowed to a stop. The bigger of the two—Sarah—turned and lifted her head, sniffing the air. Then she started to move back toward me, and Samantha followed.

"They remember you, Sarah!" Nick cried.

"Of course, they remember me! I'm their *mother*!"

They both stopped right in front of me. It looked as if they wanted to come closer but were frightened by the fluttering clothes.

"It's okay, girls, your mommy's here," I said as I reached through the line and tried to rub them behind the ears. They didn't move. They were frozen there, wanting to get closer to me but afraid of the laundry.

"Get moving, ya big dumb beasts!" Mr. McCurdy shouted.

I looked up. Two gigantic buffalo were at the top of the ramp, their heads sticking out of the trailer. A third appeared. Mr. McCurdy smacked one of them with his hat, and the buffalo jumped, its back legs kicking out behind it! Then all three came charging down the ramp, their hooves thundering and—my girls! They were right in the path of the buffalo! They'd be crushed!

"Sarah! Samantha!" I screamed.

Before I could think what to do next, Nick scrambled across the narrow corridor. He pushed the two little deer, propelling them out of the way and under the line, just as the three buffalo came charging past us, their hooves throwing up divots of grass behind them.

"Nick, are you all right!" I gasped as I grabbed him and tried to pull him to his feet.

"I'm fine...I'm okay," he said, standing. "The girls...are they all right?"

They were beside me, their little mouths working desperately to try to suckle the fingers on one of my hands.

"They're okay, too."

"That's what's important," Nick said.

"You could have gotten yourself killed!" I yelled. He would have been just as dead as the deer if a buffalo had trampled him or kicked him in the head.

"But I *didn't*, now did I?"

"But you could have."

"If I didn't do it, the girls would have been killed," Nick argued.

I shook my head. "That was just about the most stubborn, unthinking, stupid, bone-headed, brave thing I've ever seen," I said, reaching over, throwing my arms around his shoulders, and giving him a kiss on the cheek.

"Why'd you do that?" Nick demanded, wiping away my kiss with the back of his hand.

"I just wanted to thank you," I said.

"Next time you really want to thank me, don't give me a kiss. Give me cash."

I bent down and put an arm around each little deer. They snuggled into me and began to lick my face. At least somebody thought it was okay to kiss me.

"Peanuts!" Nick shouted.

I glanced up. Vladimir was leading the elephant out of the trailer. They started down the ramp, and it sagged badly under the weight of the big man and the much bigger animal. It looked as if it might break, and then they reached the safety of the grass.

"Can I ride him?" Nick yelled as he rushed toward them.

"Nicky love Peanuts! Come, come, ride elephant!" Vladimir grabbed Nick, effortlessly lifted him off the ground, and tossed him on top of the elephant.

Nick's face broke into a huge smile. Vladimir wasn't joking about Nick loving Peanuts. That's all he'd spoken about for days. In fact, he'd been talking about it so much that a couple of times I'd wanted to tell him to put a sock in it, but I didn't. Riding Peanuts at camp had been one of the highlights of Nick's summer—maybe his whole life. Now Peanuts was going to be living right next door.

"Nicky, you 'member maybe commands to make elephant go and do things?" Vladimir asked.

"Do birds fly?" Nick asked.

Vladimir shrugged. "Some birds fly. Others no fly. Penguins swim and ostrich run." Vladimir's English was pretty good, but he still missed some things, especially humour or sarcasm.

"Does Nicky remember?" Vladimir asked again.

"Yes, of course," Nick answered.

Nick leaned forward and put his head by one of the elephant's big ears. He said something, not loud enough for me to hear, but obviously loud enough for the elephant. Peanuts performed a little bow, and Vladimir clapped his hands in appreciation.

"Do you fellas think you could wait till all the animals are safe before you start playing around?" Mr. McCurdy barked from the back of the trailer.

"Trailer empty and—"

"The buffalo!" Nick screamed.

I turned around. The three big buffalo had come back out of the pen and were pushing up against the lines. They were trying to get away!

Vladimir rushed toward the buffalo, yelling and waving his hands. All three of the beasts turned to face him. He'd gotten their attention, but instead of running back into the pen, they just stared at him. One of them—the big male—began to paw the ground! Was it going to charge him?

Vladimir skidded to a stop. Thank goodness he wasn't going to butt heads with the buffalo.

"Nicky!" Vladimir yelled. "Make elephant come forward... charge at buffalo!"

"Nicholas, no!" I cried. "You can't—"

My words were lost in the pounding of Peanuts' feet against the ground as he lumbered straight at the buffalo. The buffalo spun around, and all three of them galloped through the opening and back into the pen. Vladimir jumped in front of the elephant, and Peanuts stopped at the entrance.

"Good boy, Peanuts! Good boy, Nicky!" Vladimir called out. He quickly took the roll of fencing and started sealing off the opening to trap the animals inside. Mr. McCurdy hurried over—I was always amazed at how fast those old legs of his could move when they needed to. In a matter of minutes he had the fencing in place and had used metal ties to secure it.

I walked over, and the two little deer—bigger than they had been just two weeks ago—bounced into the back of my legs and almost knocked me over. I regained my balance and went to Mr. McCurdy's side.

"We were lucky those buffalo were afraid of Peanuts," Nick said.

"All buffalo 'fraid of bigger buffalo and elephant is just bigger buffalo to them," Vladimir said.

"I thought Peanuts was going in there, too," I said.

"*Nyet*," Vladimir said. "Pen no good for Peanuts. He would no like and just walk through fence. Peanuts stay other place."

"How about my house?" Nick suggested. "We have a two-car garage and only one car and—"

"I was thinking the barn would be plenty good for Peanuts," Mr. McCurdy said.

"With Buddha?" I questioned.

"He can be up on the main level. Plenty of straw and a big open space he can have all to himself."

"Is that floor strong enough to hold him?" I asked. There were places where it seemed to sag even under my weight.

"There's a couple of spots that need to be shored up."

"What about the holes in the roof and the missing boards?" I questioned.

"Neither of those is a problem for now. We'll fix 'em up before winter. He'll be okay in there. Nick, you want Vladimir to lead the elephant, or do you want to ride him to the barn?"

"You joking?" Nick asked in amazement.

Vladimir turned to me. "Big girl Sarah want to ride elephant with baby brother?"

I shook my head. "I think I'm fine just walking. Besides, I want my girls to stay with me."

"Aren't they going into the pen tonight?" Mr. McCurdy asked.

"Maybe tonight, but not right now. I want to visit with them for a while… I think they missed me."

Mr. McCurdy laughed. "I think they missed you just 'bout as much as you missed them. Bring 'em up to the house with you. We all need to get some grub."

As we strolled along the lane, I thought that if anybody was watching us, we'd make a pretty strange sight: a boy atop a large grey elephant leading the way, followed by an old man, a man as big as a bear, and a girl with two little deer. Quite the parade.

"Nicky!" Vladimir yelled. "Slow Peanuts down!" He did seem to be getting quite a bit ahead of us.

"I'm trying!" Nick shouted back over his shoulder. "He isn't listening!"

It looked as if they were pulling even farther away from us. The elephant wasn't moving his legs very fast, but his strides were so large that each one ate up lots of ground. He was getting farther and farther away.

"Peanuts!" Vladimir screamed as he ran to catch them.

What was happening? Why wasn't the elephant stopping? Was Nick in any danger?

"He's headed for the pond!" Mr. McCurdy called out. The pond was right beside the barn. It wasn't that large—or clean. The water was dark and had lots of greenish algae growing in it.

"He must still be thirsty," I said.

"Maybe," Mr. McCurdy replied.

We watched as the elephant picked up speed, Nick bouncing on top of him. Vladimir was chasing after them and—there was a gigantic splash as Peanuts charged into the pond!

"Nick!" I screamed. I ran as fast as my legs could carry me. Oh, my gosh…what had happened to my brother? Was he hurt? Was he trapped underneath the elephant? Had he been thrown free? Was he—and then I saw Nick. He was standing in the shallow water at the edge of the pond. Vladimir waded in and put an arm around him, helping him out of the water. Nick sat on the grass beside the pond.

"Nick, are you all right?" I cried as I rushed over and threw my arms around him.

"Will you stop with the hugging stuff?" he said, brushing me away with wet arms. He coughed loudly and spit up a little bit of water.

"Are you okay?"

"I'm fine," he said. "I just swallowed some water."

"You could have been killed!" I exclaimed.

"I'm okay, Sarah. Don't make more of this than it is. I just had a little water go down the wrong way. Haven't you ever had that happen?"

"Not when I was in a pond with an elephant. I was scared. I thought something had happened to you!"

"Something did happen. Something really cool," he said, gesturing to Peanuts. The elephant was standing in the middle of the pond with only the top of his head sticking out. He was spraying water into the air with his trunk.

"Cool? You think that was cool? You can't tell me you weren't just a little bit scared."

"Me? Scared?" he asked, sounding confused.

"Come on, Nick, you can't tell me you weren't scared. You'd have to be completely stupid not to be! Okay, maybe you *are* stupid enough not to be scared."

Nick snorted. "You're just saying that because you're jealous."

"Jealous!" I yelled. "Jealous of what?"

"You didn't get to go in the pond with Peanuts."

"Did you hit your head or something?"

He smiled. "It was like being on a ride at an amusement park. You know, like Mr. Elephant's Wild Ride, except for real. It was *so* cool."

I turned to Vladimir. "Why did Peanuts do that?"

"Peanuts smell water and need to drink more and get cool,"

Vladimir said. "Too hot in trailer for Peanuts. Poor elephant."

"Everybody okay?" Mr. McCurdy asked as he finally reached us.

"Nicky good, Peanuts good," Vladimir said.

Mr. McCurdy reached down and patted Nick on the head. "Take more than an elephant to crack a coconut as thick as this one."

Peanuts certainly looked good. And happy. I didn't know if elephants could smile, but it appeared as if he were smiling. He kept dipping his trunk into the water and spraying it into the air.

"Do you know what I'd like to do now?" Nick asked.

"Take a bath to get rid of the slime, change clothes, and eat?" I asked.

"That would be good, but I'd like to do one thing first." He paused, and a big grin split his face. "I'd like to try that ride one more time, but this time I'd try to stay on top of the elephant when he hit the water."

Vladimir and Mr. McCurdy burst into laughter—one a deep, booming laugh, the other a raspy, cackling chuckle. The terrible thing was I was pretty sure Nick was just joking around, but I wasn't one hundred percent certain.

Chapter 5

I looked up from my book to see a car coming up the driveway. It was a sleek, sporty, red number with tinted windows. I closed the book and put it on the chair as I got up. I'd been feeling guilty, anyway, reading while everybody else was busy working, but somebody had to watch Peanuts. He'd shown no willingness to leave the pond, and until he was out and put away in the barn, somebody had to be there. My two deer, who had been lying on the grass beside me, got up and trailed after me.

The car stopped right behind the second of the big trucks. I wondered who it could be. The door opened, and Mom stepped out. She'd mentioned she'd have to rent a car while ours was being fixed. Pretty snazzy. I waved to her, and she started walking in my direction. I met her partway. I'd still be able to keep an eye on Peanuts from there.

"So these are your girls," she said.

"These are them. The big one—this one—is Sarah, and the other is Samantha."

"They're beautiful, and a lot bigger than I expected them to be."

"They're a lot bigger than *I* thought they were going to be. They've really grown over the past couple of weeks."

"They seem pretty attached to you," Mom said.

"Shouldn't babies be attached to their mother?" I asked.

"I always thought that was the way it should be," she said with a smile. "I assume Mr. McCurdy must be here. Did he come with those trucks?"

"They held the animals. Mr. McCurdy drove one and Vladimir the other."

"It's nice he's home earlier than expected. Does that mean you and Nick will be coming home tonight?"

"We'll be home for the night, but we'll have to be right back here tomorrow. There's a lot of work to be done."

She crinkled her face. "It didn't look like you were working too hard."

"I wasn't working hard, but I was working," I assured her.

"And just what were you doing that would qualify as work?"

"I was watching—I *am* watching—Peanuts."

"Peanuts...Peanuts the elephant?" She'd heard Nick talking about the elephant enough to know it by name.

I nodded. "He's right over there in the pond."

Mom walked with me to the edge of the water. Peanuts was still almost completely submerged. All that was sticking out of the water was the very tip of his trunk. He was using it sort of like a snorkel to breathe while staying underwater.

"There's an elephant under there?" Mom asked.

"A big elephant."

"Why is he in the pond?"

"Elephants like water. He was hot and thirsty after being in the trailer, and I guess he just wanted to go for a swim." I knew better—a lot better—than to tell her who was on top of the elephant when he took his dip. I just hoped Nick was smart enough to keep that little piece of information to himself, as well. If he didn't, that might be his last ride on the elephant.

"How long has he been in there?" she asked.

I looked at my watch. It was almost five o'clock. "About four hours."

"And how long will he *be* in there?"

"I guess that's up to Peanuts."

"I see. Where's your brother and Mr. McCurdy?"

"They're in the barn with Vladimir, getting things ready."

"Ready for what?"

"Ready to transfer the cats from the trailer to their new pens," I said.

"Is that going to happen today?" She sounded anxious, as if she didn't want to be here if it was going to happen now. She probably didn't want Nick or me to be here, either.

"They need to have more materials to get the pens ready before they move the animals. I don't think that'll happen until tomorrow at the earliest. Speaking of early, why are you here so early?"

"I brought dinner for you and Nick." She held up a bag. "Chinese."

"That's great. Is there enough for Mr. McCurdy and Vladimir?" I asked.

"I didn't know they'd be here, or I would have brought more. Maybe since Mr. McCurdy is here, I can take the two of you home to eat. Or the four of you could share."

"I think I'd rather eat here and—four of us? What about you?"

"I'm not going to be eating with you. I have to meet some-body for dinner."

"A business meeting on a Friday night?" I asked.

"Not business. It's sort of a date."

"Sort of a date? Is it or isn't it a date, and with who?"

"It's nothing really. Martin invited me to join him for dinner."

"You're going to dinner with the captain—I mean, the acting chief?"

"Is there anything wrong with that?" she asked. "He seems like a nice man."

"Sure, he seems nice, but he's the acting chief of police," I explained.

"So?"

"So I don't know." It just didn't seem right. Did policemen go out on dates? Did they eat?

"Maybe I should say hello to Mr. McCurdy," Mom said. "And I'm eager to meet Vladimir before I go."

"They're in the barn. How about if you go down and get them? I'll stay here with Peanuts and—"

"Hey!" Nick yelled, coming up the path. Mr. McCurdy, Vladimir, and Calvin were right behind him. There was something about seeing a chimpanzee ambling along that always brought a smile to my face. "Have you seen my elephant?" Nick called out.

"I've seen parts of the elephant," Mom said, ignoring the part about it being *Nick's* elephant.

"How are you doing, Ellen?" Mr. McCurdy said.

"I'm doing fine, Angus. And you?" she asked as she gave him a hug.

"Good as can be." He paused. "Now where are my manners? Ellen, this is Vladimir."

Vladimir stepped forward, bowed slightly, and they shook hands. "Most pleased to meet. I am Vladimir…Vladimir Markov."

"Pleased to meet you. I'm Ellen Fraser."

Vladimir still held my mother's hand. "Fraser, like in last name of big girl Sarah and Nicky?"

"We share the same last name because I'm their mother."

"No, cannot be!" Vladimir said. "Cannot be mother…too young."

My mother looked as if she was blushing.

"But could be big sister of big girl Sarah. Look like big girl Sarah. *Pretty* like big girl Sarah." Now I felt myself start to blush.

"That's kind of you to say, Mr. Markov."

"Not Mr. Markov…Vladimir! Must call me Vladimir!"

"And you can call me Ellen."

"And now Vladimir know you are mother of wonderful big girl Sarah and Nicky I no want to just shake hands!" Vladimir pulled my mother toward him and wrapped his arms around her, lifted her off the ground, and gave her a big kiss on first one cheek and then the other. He released her. She looked completely shocked. Vladimir turned to Mr. McCurdy. "Is fine to hug and kiss women, no?"

"A lot better than hugging me," Mr. McCurdy said, cackling.

"Good, good." He turned back to my mother. "Your kids is wonderful! Smart, kind, care for animals! Very brave and—"

"Brave?" she asked.

"Very brave!"

The last thing I wanted was for him to tell our mother anything more than she needed to know about what had happened at the animal camp.

"He means around animals," I said, butting in. "You know how we're not afraid of animals—especially Nick."

She nodded but didn't look convinced. I thought I'd better change the subject before she asked anything more, or Vladimir volunteered something.

"Mom brought us dinner," I said, pointing at the plastic bag she was still holding. Mentioning food always seemed to distract people.

"Food, all right! What did you bring?" Nick asked as he tried to look in the bag.

"Chinese food, but I'm afraid I didn't bring enough. I didn't know Angus was back with Mr. Mar—Vladimir."

"But we can share what you brought, and I can make up something to go along with it for all of us," I said.

"That's okay, Sarah. We wouldn't want to be any troub—" Mr. McCurdy began.

"The only trouble would be if you didn't eat with us. We're sharing and that's that!" I stated loudly.

Mr. McCurdy looked as if he was going to argue but didn't.

Vladimir shrugged. "Vladimir not argue about food. Important thing not what is eaten but who it eaten with." He paused. "Will big girl Sarah's mommy be eating with us?"

"Not tonight," she said. "I have a previous engagement."

"Engagement?" Vladimir asked. "What is engagement?"

"Sort of like a date," I said.

"Big girl Sarah's mommy have date? She have boyfriend?"

"Not a boyfriend," she said. "I'm just having dinner with somebody."

"With who?" Nick asked.

"The acting chief of police," I said.

"You're eating with him?" Nick gasped.

"Why do my children seem so surprised by that?"

"Well, he does seem mighty old for you," Mr. McCurdy said. "He's practically my age."

"Not the *old* chief," my mother explained. "The new chief is the old captain."

"So they finally replaced that old bird."

"He's retiring, and the captain replaced him," I said. "It's not official yet, so he's still the *acting* chief for another couple of months."

"He seemed like a decent enough fella…especially there at the end. You want the kids to stay here tonight?" Mr. McCurdy asked.

"No, they might as well sleep at home," Mom said.

"It's just if you're going to be out really late—"

"I won't be out that late," she said. "We're just having dinner. I'll be home early enough to tuck them both into bed."

I didn't really want to be tucked in by anybody, but it would be good to be home in my own bed tonight—and have her there with us.

Mom looked at her watch. "In fact, we're having an early dinner, so I should go home, have a shower, change, and get to the restaurant." She was standing with her back toward the pond, and as she stood there, Peanuts stuck his head out of the water and began to emerge slowly.

"Do you want to see all the new animals before you go?" Nick asked.

"I'd like to, but I don't think I have time right now."

Nick, who was standing beside me, could see Peanuts as well as I could. "How about if you just see one animal, one *big* animal?"

Peanuts continued to move. Vladimir and Mr. McCurdy were facing away, as well, so it was only Nick and me who could see Peanuts. Maybe I should have said something so she wasn't startled. Maybe I shouldn't.

"I'd love to, Nick, but I really don't want to rush things. How about if I drive the two of you back here tomorrow? Then I'll have time to see the animals—"

My mother was blasted in the back of the head by a stream of filthy water that Peanuts sprayed out of his trunk! She staggered forward, practically falling! Vladimir reached out and grabbed her, stopping her from tumbling over.

"Bad elephant!" Vladimir yelled.

Peanuts trumpeted, sounding like something out of a Tarzan movie. My mother turned around, saw the elephant, and jumped backward, away from him.

"Very bad elephant!" Vladimir waved his hands and started toward Peanuts, who retreated into the water. He went deeper and deeper until only his trunk and the top of his head were sticking out of the water again.

I looked at my mother. Her hair was plastered to her head and her clothes—at least the back of her clothes—were soaked. That wasn't good. She was wearing one of her court outfits, an expensive tailored black skirt suit. Maybe it was ruined. Hopefully it just needed to be dry-cleaned.

"Are you okay, Mom?" I asked.

"I'm...I'm...an elephant just spit at me."

"No, no, it didn't spit. It sort of sprayed," I tried to explain.

She shook her head, wide-eyed. "No, something that was in its mouth is now all over me."

"Not really his mouth," I said. "I guess it's really more like his nose."

"And that's better?" she gasped. The expression on her face showed just how disgusted she felt. "Wipe that smile off your face!" she said, pointing at Nick. There was a smirk there that instantly faded.

"I wasn't smiling...honestly. I was just thinking that Peanuts probably did that because he likes you."

"Because he likes me?" Mom asked. She sounded as shocked by what he had said as she was by the original blast of water.

"Yeah. Maybe he did that because he was sort of giving you a present," Nick said. "Does that make sense, Vladimir?"

Now it was Vladimir's turn to seem confused. He shook his head. "Elephants very smart animals. No give filthy water as present."

"Then why would he do that?" my mother asked.

Vladimir shrugged. "Maybe he just think it funny."

"Well, I certainly don't think it's funny," she said.

"Either way, though, it did save you some time," Nick said.

"Time?"

"Yeah, thanks to Peanuts you won't have to take a shower before your date."

Suddenly I burst into laughter. I couldn't help myself. I tried to stifle it, but it just came out. My mother looked like a drowned rat in a business suit. Mr. McCurdy cackled, Vladimir chuckled, Nick laughed, and then even my mother cracked a smile—a little one, but it was still a smile.

Chapter 6

"But you said you'd come and see the animals this morning," Nick said as Mom drove way too fast up Mr. McCurdy's bumpy driveway. I held on to the edge of the seat with both hands to keep from bouncing in the air.

"I wish I could, but I'm late for work."

"But you promised," Nick insisted.

"I know, but I wasn't planning on sleeping in when I made that promise."

"You wouldn't have slept in if you hadn't been out so late last night," Nick snapped. Mom hadn't gotten in until a lot later than she'd originally thought. We'd been "tucked in" long before she came home.

Mom stopped the car behind one of the trucks. It was blocking her from driving any farther. "I've already apologized for that," she said. "I didn't mean to be so late last night, but I just lost track of the time."

"I'm surprised you could even fit behind the wheel of this little car to drive us," Nick said. "Any meal that lasted for four hours must have put a lot of weight on you. Is that why you were so late? Because you had to digest the food before you could drive home?"

"Nick, we did a lot more than eat."

"What do you mean by that?" Nick demanded angrily.

"We talked. We talked for hours! I had no idea that the two of us had so much in common."

"You have a lot in common with the acting chief?" Nick asked in amazement.

"Why does that surprise you so much?" she asked. "Lawyers and police officers have a lot in common."

"The only thing I can see is that he arrests crooks, and you try to get them off. That hardly seems like a good thing to have in common," Nick argued.

"Nick, give it a rest," I said. "Come on, let's get to work." I started to get out of the car, stopped, and glanced at Mom. "You're only going to work for a few hours, right?"

"Just a half day. I'll be back to see the animals in a few hours."

"That's great," I said.

"Yeah, we'll see you then, I guess," Nick said. "Unless you run into somebody else you've got so much in common with that you forget we're here."

"Nicky, please don't be like that," Mom begged.

He slammed the car door and walked away without answering her.

"I'll talk to him," I offered. "He'll be okay."

"Thank you, Sarah." She leaned across the car and gave me a kiss on the cheek. "I can always count on you."

"We'll see you this afternoon, right?" I asked.

"No question."

I was going to close the door when I hesitated. "You like him, don't you?"

"Of course I like him! He can be a little bit annoying at times, as you well know, but he's my son—"

"I didn't mean Nick."

"Oh, you mean Martin."

I nodded.

"He does seem very nice."

"Are you going to see him again?" I asked.

"I hope…but we'll see. He said he'd call. I hope he does."

"If he's smart, he'll call, and if he doesn't, he's stupid. You don't want a stupid person to call, anyway," I said. "So, either way, there's nothing to worry about."

"Sarah, you're such a sweetheart. I really appreciate all your support and encouragement, although at times it makes me feel a little guilty."

"Guilty?"

"Yes, guilty. Here I am, the mother, and you're the one offering me words of encouragement. Shouldn't I be the one helping you deal with insecurities and self-esteem issues around dating and boys and—"

"That's okay," I said, cutting her off before she could say anything else that might be even more embarrassing.

"You know, if you have any questions about boys, I'd be more than willing to listen—"

"I don't have any questions. None. Period."

"Sarah, it's okay to ask questions. You're a young lady, and it's quite natural for you to be aware of boys."

"I'm aware of them," I said. "I'm aware that most of them are seriously stupid."

My mother let out a big sigh. "Sarah, just because your father made some bad decisions in leaving us, doesn't mean that most males are stupid."

"I didn't say that!" I protested.

"It's okay to be mad at him."

"I'm not mad at him!" I snapped. That was at least only half a lie. I wasn't as mad at him as I had been when he left us—it had been over a year now. Time heals all wounds. I'd read that someplace. Of course, I'd have to live to be around two hundred years old before I was completely free of all that anger.

"It's just I've noticed that sometimes you treat males like

they're little boys."

"What males have you seen me around?" I asked.

"Well, sometimes you don't treat Nicholas very well."

"Nicholas *is* a little boy! My little brother! And he *is* stupid most of the time, like he's being now!"

"It's just that sometimes you have an attitude around males. Like you think they're going to show bad judgement."

"I don't act like that!"

"You often did with your father."

"That's because he *was* showing bad judgement!"

"I thought you weren't mad at him?" my mother said.

I took a deep breath. There was nothing worse than having a mother who was a lawyer—except having a mother who was a lawyer who was getting ready for a big trial. "I *was* mad at him, back then. Now I'm not. And I don't want to talk about it anymore."

My mother looked as if she wanted to say more, but she didn't. She was waiting for me to speak, and that wasn't going to happen.

"I should get going now, I guess," Mom said.

"Yeah...see you later."

I climbed out and closed the door. Mom jockeyed the car back and forth a few times so she could turn around in the narrow lane behind the truck. It certainly was a big truck—wait—where was the second truck? Mom honked as she started up the lane, and I waved to her, then hurried off to the house. Not only did I want to talk to Nick, but I wanted to know who was gone and where he'd taken the truck.

I knocked on the door and then entered. Mr. McCurdy had told us to feel free to walk in, but it always felt better to announce I was coming. I found Nick sitting at the kitchen table with Calvin. The chimp was eating out of one of the Chinese food containers from last night. I'd made so much to go along with the Chinese food that there was still some left over. Even though Calvin was only using his fingers instead of utensils, I couldn't help notice he was still less messy in his eating habits than my brother.

"Is Mr. McCurdy here?" I asked.

"I'm in here, Sarah," he called from another room. I was always amazed at how well he could hear when he wanted to.

"What happened to the second truck?" I yelled out. "Did Vladimir take it some—"

"No need to holler, Sarah," Mr. McCurdy said, walking into the room.

"Sorry. Did Vladimir take the truck?"

"Yep."

"Where did he go to?"

"To the dump."

"What's he dropping off?"

"He's not dropping off. He's picking up."

"At the dump?"

"Sure. We need lots of things to make the pens for the cats, and people dump off lots of good stuff," Mr. McCurdy said.

"Stuff you can use to make a cage?"

"That's where I got all the things to convert Buddha's cattle stall into a cage."

"I guess it's good we're here to help. What can we do?" I asked.

He turned to my brother. "Nick, are you through with the Chinese food?"

"We're all done," Nick said. Both he and Calvin were sitting at the table wearing empty containers of Chinese food on their heads like hats. I certainly hoped they were finished.

"I want you to go down to the barn and get enough chickens for all the cats in the trailer."

"I don't know if I can carry that many," Nick said.

"Bring the chimp. He could practically carry the whole freezer."

Nick stood. "Come on, Calvin, let's go." The two of them started off.

"Goodbye, stupid boy!" Polly called out as they left the room.

I looked at the parrot sitting on top of the cupboards. "That wasn't nice, Polly," I said.

"Shut up, stupid girl," Polly squawked.

Mr. McCurdy chuckled.

"Even if you think I'm stupid, Polly, I still think you're smart," I said. I'd decided I wasn't going to get into any arguments with a parrot. No matter what that parrot said to me, I'd just compliment him back.

"Ugly girl," Polly said.

"You're a pretty bird, Polly."

"Stupid, ugly girl," Polly squawked.

Mr. McCurdy laughed. "Believe me, Sarah, it doesn't make any more sense for you to reason with him than it does for Nick to argue with him. Just let him be, okay?"

"I was just trying to—"

Suddenly the back door blew open. "Help! Help!" Nick screamed as he ran down the hall, screeching to a halt in front of us. "The buffalo have gotten out!"

"What are you talking about?" Mr. McCurdy demanded.

"The buffalo have broken out of the pen!"

"Are you sure?"

"Of course I'm sure! I just saw them walking up the lane as I was going to the trailer to feed the cats!"

"Come on," Mr. McCurdy said as he headed for the door. Nick rushed down the hall past him, and I ran to keep up. We'd hardly gotten out the door when I caught sight of the buffalo. The three of them were behind the trailer, slowly ambling down the driveway. Calvin was sitting beside the trailer, a couple of feed buckets at his side.

"What are we going to do?" I asked.

"We're going to get them back in their pen. But first we have to make sure none of the other animals escaped."

"Like my girls!" I ran up the lane toward the pen. "Sarah!

Samantha!" I yelled. The buffalo were on the lane on the other side of the pen, and as I rushed forward they startled and began racing away from me. I shouldn't have run. And I shouldn't have been yelling. They disappeared around a bend in the lane. Luckily it was a long driveway. There was still quite a distance to go before they'd reach the road.

"Nice going, Sarah," Nick said, voicing what I already knew.

"I didn't mean to scare them. I didn't think...I was thinking about my girls."

Mr. McCurdy walked up after us. "Forget the buffalo for now. We've got to repair the leak in the bottle before we try to put any more water into it."

"What does that mean?" Nick asked.

"It means we've got to fix whatever way they got out to stop the others from leaving and to make sure the buffalo don't get back out that way again after we've caught them," Mr. McCurdy explained.

We followed him as he cut across the field toward the pen. At first I couldn't see much—were any of the deer still inside the enclosure? As we got closer, I caught sight of a deer at the far end among the trees. Then I saw another and another and another. I spotted both of my babies. I did a quick head count. All the deer were still in the pen. Thank goodness! It became apparent how the buffalo had escaped. The place where they'd entered the pen—where the fence had been tied together—was open. The hole wasn't big, but it was large enough to let out a buffalo. There were big black clumps of buffalo fur all along that section of the fence. The buffalo were still shedding parts of their thick winter coats.

"I figure the buffalo weren't even trying to get out," Mr. McCurdy said. "Probably just rubbing up against the fence 'cause they felt itchy and pushed so hard they snapped off the straps holding the fence together.

"We can fix that," Nick said. "Put on a lot more straps to

make it tighter. I can do it."

"Not now." Mr. McCurdy said. "We just put on a couple of straps, so the deer don't get out, but we can open it up fast to get the buffalo back inside when we drive 'em back this way. Does that make sense?"

"A lot of sense," Nick said. "Except for the part about driving them back. How exactly are we going to do that?"

"Shovels," I said under my breath.

"Shovels?" Nick exclaimed. "We're going to shovel them back?"

"No, of course not! But we're going to use shovels and rakes. Remember at the camp how you waved around a rake so we could go into the pen and help the deer without the buffalo charging us?"

"Of course I remember," Nick said.

We'd had to go into the pen with Vladimir when my little deer were being born because their mother was having trouble. We'd waved shovels in the air to keep the buffalo at the far end of the pen. If it had worked there, it should work here…shouldn't it?

"Mr. McCurdy, your tools are all down in the barn, aren't they?" I asked.

"Pretty much."

"Nick, go and get a couple of shovels and a rake and come back fast," I said.

"What will you two be doing?" Nick asked.

"We'll fix the opening and then work our way down the road to find the buffalo. Then we'll all drive them back," Mr. McCurdy said.

"Sounds like a plan to me," Nick said, and he hurried down the lane to the barn.

Mr. McCurdy picked up a piece of metal from the ground— one of the straps that had popped off under the weight of the buffalo. He muscled the fence into place and began tying the two sections together. Bending down, I grabbed two more pieces of the strapping and handed them to him. He secured those in place, as well.

"Let's go and do a little buffalo hunting."

As we started up the lane, Calvin came over and joined us. He grabbed Mr. McCurdy's hand.

"Where's that brother of yours?" Mr. McCurdy demanded.

"He should be here soon."

"He should be here now!" Mr. McCurdy snapped. "We don't have time to wait for him. Let's get going."

We walked quickly along the lane, Calvin still holding on to Mr. McCurdy's hand. If things hadn't been so serious, I would have laughed at the sight of the two of them.

We took the first bend in the lane, but the buffalo were nowhere to be seen. I scanned the fields, first one side and then the other. If they hadn't left the driveway, they had to be farther along—closer to the road.

"The farther they get, the farther we have to drive them back," Mr. McCurdy said. "I wish Vladimir was here."

"So do I. He's big enough that he could practically pick up the buffalo and carry them back."

"But not all at once," Mr. McCurdy said. "He'd have to make at least three separate trips to carry—"

His words were cut off by the sound of a car horn blaring. Mr. McCurdy looked at me, and I knew we were both thinking the same thing. The road was just up ahead, and the buffalo must be on it.

"We'd better hurry," he said.

We doubled our pace up the bumpy and rutted lane. Calvin let go of Mr. McCurdy's hand so he could use both of his arms—knuckles on the ground—to keep up with us.

There was a swooshing noise and a flash of colour as a car sped past the driveway along the road. I listened closely, holding my breath, hoping that sound wouldn't be followed by either a honk or a crash. Nothing. We reached the road. There, up the road, were the buffalo. Two, the female cows, were grazing in the grass at the side while the third, the big male, was standing defiantly in the middle of the gravel road. That car must have had to edge over to one side to get by the big bison.

"What do we do now?" I asked.

"Me and Calvin are going to sneak through the field so we can get on the other side of the buffalo."

"What do I do?"

"You just move that way a dozen or so feet," Mr. McCurdy said, pointing down the road in the opposite direction from where the buffalo were.

All at once I felt relieved and disappointed. "But I want to help."

"You will be helping," he said.

"How will I be helping by getting out of the way?"

"You don't understand, Sarah. Once Calvin and me get to the far side of the buffalo, we're going to try to drive 'em back in this direction, and that's where you come in."

"Me?"

He nodded. "You're going to scare 'em into going down the driveway instead of farther along the road."

"Me? I'm going to do that by myself?" I sputtered.

"Hopefully not. By the time we work our way around to the far side, I'm thinking Nick'll be here. So the two of you and a couple of shovels are going to drive those buffalo back down the driveway. Understand?"

I nodded dumbly in agreement. I certainly understood what he had in mind. Doing it was a different thing entirely. He wanted me—and Nick if he'd hurry up and get here—to stand in the middle of the road and direct a stampeding herd of buffalo. Gee, that certainly didn't seem difficult. Nearly impossible, yes, difficult, no.

Startled by the sound of a vehicle, I turned in time to see a car speeding up the road toward the buffalo and me. I waved my arms to get the driver's attention. He slowed down, and I moved to the side of the road so he could pass. The driver stopped beside me and rolled down his window.

"Wow, I've seen a lot of cows get loose around here and get to the road, but this is a first—a buffalo," he said.

"Well, this is the first time they've gotten loose," I answered. Of course, that was the truth, because today was the first time they'd ever been here.

"Is it safe for me to drive by?" he asked.

At least two other cars that I knew of had driven by. "Sure, I guess."

"Good luck rounding them up," he said.

He drove slowly forward, going to the far side of the road, away from the two buffalo grazing in the grass, and giving the big guy in the centre as wide a berth as he could. That went okay. Now, if my brother could just get here so I wouldn't be alone.

Off to the side, in the field, I caught sight of Mr. McCurdy and Calvin. They were making a big circle around the buffalo, trying not to be noticed until they came out on the far side. It wouldn't take them long to get into position and start driving the buffalo back toward me. A shiver went up my spine. *Please, Nick, stop whatever you're doing and get here,* I thought. *I promise I won't yell at you for taking so long. Just get here as fast as you can—* I stopped mid-thought as I saw Nick coming up the lane. He was riding on the back of Peanuts!

I was hit by a wave of confused thoughts and emotions. I didn't know whether to feel grateful, upset, angry, shocked, or surprised. So I was all of them at once.

Nick waved at me, and even from that distance I could see that he was smiling. How stupid was he being? We needed him to drive the buffalo back into the pen, and he was selfishly taking this opportunity to joyride on the elephant and—of course! How stupid was *I* being? Nick was bringing the elephant to help. The buffalo were afraid of Peanuts, and Nick had used Peanuts to drive them into the pen in the first place, so he could do the same thing now. Rather than it just being me, or even me and Nick trying to drive the buffalo down the lane, now it was Nick, an elephant, and me! This just might work.

"Ya! Get moving!" Mr. McCurdy yelled.

I looked over. He and Calvin were on the road on the far side of the buffalo. He was screaming and yelling and flapping his arms, trying to drive the buffalo toward me. But Nick wasn't here yet! He was still down the lane! Mr. McCurdy hadn't seen him, and if the buffalo got to the lane before Nick got out on the road, he'd just drive them farther away.

"Get moving!" Mr. McCurdy shouted.

The biggest buffalo turned to face him, stubbornly not moving. It began to paw at the ground as if it were going to charge him. This wasn't good. This was terrible! Mr. McCurdy was too old to be dodging a charging buffalo.

A car appeared on the road behind Mr. McCurdy. It was small and blue and moving at a tremendous pace. The driver bounced up the road, saw him, swerved, slammed on the brakes, and screeched to a stop, just missing him!

The big buffalo spun around and began to run in my direction. The other two joined in. All three were racing toward me! Oh, my God!

"Hurry up, Nick!" I screamed in desperation.

I glanced up. The buffalo were still coming forward. Mr. McCurdy and Calvin were yelping and waving their arms, driving them. The buffalo reached the lane and started down it but skidded to a stop at the sight of the elephant lumbering toward them. They'd gotten there before Nick had. All three buffalo turned and galloped back the way they'd come. This was awful—Peanuts wasn't forcing them toward the pen, but away from it! Nick and Peanuts came out onto the road right behind the buffalo. Now there were three buffalo and one elephant on the road!

Then, behind Mr. McCurdy, another car appeared. It slowed down and came to a stop. Almost before the wheels had ceased spinning, a man jumped out of the driver's door. He had a camera in his hand and began frantically snapping pictures. A tow truck pulled up behind the car. What was happening here? There were never this many vehicles on this section of road. It was like a traffic jam in the middle of a deserted country road.

I heard the noise of another car. This one was coming from behind me. I heard it but couldn't see it over the crest of the road. Then it appeared. It was a shiny white car, and it practically jumped off the road as it headed over the rise and barrelled forward, bearing down on us! Could it stop in time before hitting one of the other cars, or the buffalo?

A cloud of dust flew up as the driver hit the brakes and the car spun around. It was suddenly facing the wrong direction, then back around, then the wrong direction again, and then it slid into the ditch at the side of the road. That wasn't great, but at least it had stopped and—oh, no—it was a police car!

Chapter 7

The captain—the acting chief—leaped out of his car and climbed onto the road. I had to fight the urge to sink deeper into the other ditch and out of his sight. But no matter how much I wanted to do that I couldn't. I rushed toward him.

"Are you all right?" I asked.

"I'm fine," he said calmly—a lot more calmly than I'd have been if my car had just done a three-sixty and I'd ended up in the ditch after almost running into a herd of buffalo and an elephant.

"What about your car?"

"The car's fine. That's what you call a controlled skid."

"You mean you meant to put it in the ditch?"

"I meant not to hit anything. The ditch was better than hitting something else. More importantly, is Nick okay? Do we need to help him get off that elephant?"

"Oh, no, Nick's fine. He's using the elephant to help herd the buffalo. We have to get them back onto Mr. McCurdy's farm and into their pen."

"It doesn't look like Nick's having much luck."

That was an understatement. Nick and Peanuts were chasing the buffalo all around the road, but they kept skittering away, breaking off on their own and then reforming as a little herd again. It looked like a strange animal square dance. Nick kept chasing them, but they weren't going anywhere near the lane. The only thing keeping them from running away were the ditches and fences on both sides of the road and the backup of cars blocking the road itself in both directions. Where had all these vehicles come from? There were two cars blocking the way in one direction. The other way there were two cars and two tow trucks. Just then a third tow truck appeared with its lights blazing. It certainly wouldn't take three tow trucks to get one police car out of the ditch. There was no point in all three of them being here unless they thought the buffalo or the elephant were going to damage a car, which could happen. A charging buffalo could easily put a dent in the side of a car, and I didn't even want to think about what would happen if Peanuts stomped on a vehicle. Nick and Peanuts continued to charge around after the buffalo, and I suddenly saw the cars as not just blocking them but being in danger.

At least everybody was staying in their cars—except the guy with the camera. He was still running around snapping pictures.

"That guy should get back into his car before he gets hurt," I said, gesturing toward him.

"He's just trying to do his job."

"His job?"

"He's with the newspaper. Don't you recognize him? He's the guy that took the picture of you and Nick with Buddha last year that ended up in papers across the country."

"That's him?"

"That's him, but I guess you really didn't get a very good look at him, did you? After all, if you remember, you were *under* the tiger just after he took that shot."

Being under a tiger is one of those things you don't forget. His flash had startled Buddha, and he'd almost broken free, dragging me along with him.

"How does he always know when to show up?" I asked.

"Same way I knew. He's listening in on the police radio calls."

"This was on the police radio?" I asked in shock.

"A car driver called it in, and then it came over the radio asking me to investigate. The tow truck drivers and news photographer must have picked it up over the radio. They're always monitoring our calls, looking for a little action. These news outlets try to find out what we're up to so they can—oh, great!"

"What? What's wrong?" I asked apprehensively.

"We've got more company."

"Where?" I looked around. "I didn't see anybody else drive up."

"Not drive. Fly," he said, pointing skyward.

Coming across the field was a helicopter! "What's a helicopter doing here?"

"If I'm not mistaken, that's the traffic chopper for the local television studio."

"It's coming to cover this traffic jam?" I asked.

"Not the traffic jam, but what caused the problem. This must be quite a scene from up there."

I couldn't argue with that. It certainly looked pretty strange from down here, so the picture from up there would have been incredible. The helicopter swooped over us and then did a tight circle. On the side were the call letters of the station, and a television camera stuck out of an open window.

"I bet this is going to make the news tonight," the acting chief said. He suddenly began to laugh.

Was he losing it? How could he find any of this funny?

"This remind you of anything?" he asked.

How could three buffalo being chased around by my brother on the back of an elephant remind me of anything except some sort of deranged nightmare?

"Escaped animal, police, newspaper photographer...any of that seem familiar?"

Of course, this was similar to the time that Buddha escaped—the first time I'd met the captain.

"Things are a little bit different this time, though," he said.

"They are?" I didn't like the way that sounded. The last time everything eventually worked out the right way. Did he mean it wasn't going to be okay this time? "What do you mean, different?" I asked.

"Well, for one thing, this time we're all on the same side. You want my help, don't you?"

"Yes, of course."

"Good." The acting chief turned and headed to his car. He reached in and grabbed something—it was a gun!

What was he going to do with that? Was he going to shoot the buffalo? I couldn't let him do that, but I couldn't very well stop him, could I? "You can't shoot them!" I yelled.

"Shoot them?" he questioned.

"The gun," I said, pointing at his hand.

"My gun is in my holster. These are flares," he said, raising them.

Now that he held them up, it obviously it wasn't a gun, but they did have sort of a barrel like a gun.

"What are you going to use flares for?"

"You'll see. Can you get Nick and the elephant to go away?"

"I guess so."

"Good, because we're not going to be able to do anything with the two of them disturbing the buffalo like that."

I walked away from the acting chief and toward the action. I didn't want to get too close, but near enough for Nick to hear me.

"Nick!" I screamed. He didn't even turn around. I went a little bit closer. "Nick!"

He turned to face me and gave me a questioning look.

"You and Peanuts have to stop!" I yelled. "It isn't working!"

He nodded. That wasn't the response I'd expected. I thought he'd argue with me.

"Take Peanuts down the lane. When we get the buffalo back onto the farm, you can chase them back into the pen!"

"How are you going to make them go back down the lane?" he yelled back.

That was a very good question. I knew it had something to do with the flares, but I didn't exactly know what. "The acting chief has a plan," I said.

Again Nick nodded. The buffalo were on the far side of the road. The two cows had gone back to grazing while the big bull stood staring at Peanuts. Nick gave the elephant a command and he started off toward the lane, walking slowly until he disappeared around the curve. Peanuts must have been pretty happy to stop. None of this would have been particularly fun for him, either. All he probably wanted was to jump back into the pond.

I looked over to where Mr. McCurdy, Calvin, and the acting chief stood. Along with them were three other men—the drivers of the tow trucks. The acting chief handed each of them a flare. Then they fanned out until they formed a big circle on all sides of the buffalo. On cue they lit their flares and a bright sparkling light went off.

"Sarah!" Mr. McCurdy yelled. "Go down to the pen and open it up so we can drive 'em in!"

I ran toward the lane, glancing back over my shoulder. It was obvious what they were doing. They had the buffalo in the middle of the circle and were moving in on all sides, leaving only one opening—the lane. I ran faster. Those buffalo only had one place to go, and I wanted to make sure I was far away when they began to move in my direction. Besides, I had to get the pen open in time.

It wasn't long before I caught up to Nick and Peanuts. The elephant was standing in a shady spot on the lane, pulling leaves off a big maple tree with his trunk and stuffing them into his mouth.

"You have to move farther away!" I shouted to him. "The buffalo are going to be coming soon, and if you're here you'll scare them back the other way!"

Nick bent down and said something to Peanuts. At first it looked as if the big beast was ignoring him, then slowly he started to amble down the lane.

"Stop just beside the trailer!" I hollered.

On the ground were the two long pieces of clothesline. I quickly tied one end to the trailer and the other end to the fence, right beside where I was going to open it up. I didn't have time to hang anything on the lines, but maybe this would be enough to direct the buffalo where they belonged.

I looked back the way I'd come. The three buffalo were heading down the lane. It had worked! But had it worked too soon? I fumbled with the first strap holding the fence closed. It didn't want to come off! I glanced over my shoulder. The buffalo were almost at the trailer now! Right behind them were the acting chief and Mr. McCurdy, flares still in their hands, blazing away. Overhead the helicopter was still hovering. I didn't have time to worry about the chopper. I had to get the fence open!

Grabbing the fence with both hands, I pulled at it with all my might. The three straps securing it went flying into the air. I peeled the fence back to create a large opening—big enough to let in a bunch of buffalo. I hoped this would be good enough.

The buffalo galloped forward. Seeing the trailer and Peanuts blocking their way in front, a fence off to the other side, and the men with the flares coming up from behind, they broke toward the pen with the big male leading the way. It looked as if he was going to run through the clothesline when he suddenly turned left and continued along beside it. The two females followed, and all three of them ran straight into the pen!

For a split second I was so happy that I didn't move. Then I realized I had to seal up the opening so they couldn't change their minds. Bringing the fence back across the opening, I closed it.

"Good work, Sarah!" Mr. McCurdy yelled out as he and the acting chief rushed to my side. Mr. McCurdy began gathering up the straps so he could tie the two sections of fence into place. "That worked pretty darn good!" he chortled. "Darn good plan!"

The acting chief smiled. "Certainly not as exciting as chasing them around with an elephant, but I was pretty sure it would work."

"Believe me, that wasn't my idea," Mr. McCurdy protested. "Say, if I didn't know better, I would have sworn you've done that before."

"Not with buffalo," the acting chief said. "But I grew up on a dairy farm, and the cows were always getting loose. That happens on farms around here all the time. I figured what worked for cows would work for buffalo."

"It worked wonderfully," I said. "We'll make sure it doesn't happen again." I paused. "We're not in trouble, are we?"

"You're in no more trouble than those farmers whose cows get loose. You fix the fence good, though, because I wouldn't want to make this a habit."

"Doing it right now," Mr. McCurdy said. "And once the permanent pen is built that will never happen."

"Thank you so much for your help. We were lucky you were so close by," I added.

"I was actually on my way to your house," the acting chief said.

"My house?"

He nodded. "I was going to see if your mother wanted to join me for lunch."

"She's not there. She's at the office working."

"I guess that means lunch is out."

"She's free for supper," I blurted out, and then realized I maybe shouldn't have said anything.

He smiled. "Are you her social secretary?"

I felt myself blushing. "No. I just know she had me take out a roast for dinner, so she doesn't have any plans."

"It sounds like she does have plans. Plans to eat with you and your brother."

"That's okay. She can eat with us anytime."

"Well, I have an idea. Could you tell her that I'll pick all three of you up around seven?"

"All of us?" I questioned.

"Unless you or your brother have other plans."

"No…um…not really."

"Good! Then I'll see you at seven. That'll give you a chance to see yourself on the news at six."

I'd forgotten about the television helicopter, even though it was still hovering overhead.

"Wave for the camera," he said as he gave a big wave. "I'll see you later."

"I can't believe you got all this stuff from the dump," Nick said.

"Lots of stuff…good stuff. This is rich country so has rich garbage," Vladimir answered.

"I just wish it hadn't been so heavy," Nick complained.

"Metal is heavy," I said to Nick. "I guess it would have been a lot lighter if we'd been making the cages out of tissue paper."

"Very funny, Sarah. I just think it would have been a lot easier if Mr. McCurdy had let some other people stay around and help do the lugging."

A lot of our friends—Mr. McCurdy's friends—had shown up and offered to help. He'd shown them all the animals but asked everybody to leave and come back next week when everything was set up. He'd said it was better not to have so many extra bodies milling around. It was easier on the animals and safer. I didn't want to ask too much about what he meant by safer.

Vladimir was strapping the second of two old metal bed frames to the very top of one of the cattle stalls. They filled the gap between the stall and the ceiling. He grasped it with both hands and gave the top section of the cage a good shake. It moved but stayed firmly in place.

"Good…strong…hold animal."

"Which animal did you have in mind?" I asked.

"Cage for Boo Boo."

"I thought you'd build her something outside like she had before," I said.

"Will build later. First, must have place for all animals. Must build seven pens."

"Do you have enough bed frames to convert that many stalls?" I asked.

"Not many beds, but many different pieces of metal. Vladimir can do. You see."

"But I don't think we'll be able to see tonight," I said. "We have to be getting home soon."

"Why do we have to go home so early?" Nick asked.

"Well…we have sort of an appointment," I said. I hadn't told him that we had a date with the acting chief. He wasn't going to be happy about that.

"What sort of appointment?" he asked suspiciously.

I turned and faced him, put my hands on my hips, and cast him a stern look. "Are you telling me you've forgotten?" I demanded. Sometimes the best defence was a good offence.

"Well…I guess that maybe I just sort of—"

"If you don't remember, then I'm certainly not going to tell you. We have to be home by five."

"That's probably better, anyway," Mr. McCurdy piped in. He was working on a pen at the far side of the barn, right beside Buddha.

"Why?" Nick asked.

"Same reason I asked the others to leave," he explained. "Just safer."

"Is moving the cats going to be dangerous?" I asked.

"Not for me and Vladimir." Mr. McCurdy stood and walked over to where we were. "Nick, can you go up to the house and check on Calvin and Laura?"

"Laura's probably asleep," Nick said.

"It's not her I'm worrying about. That Calvin can be a real handful some days. You know, a couple of weeks ago he practically turned the kitchen upside down looking for something to eat. Can you believe that?"

Nick and I exchanged looks. "Hard to believe," Nick said. "I'll go up and check on everything."

I turned back to Mr. McCurdy. "Are you going to use the tranquillizer gun to move the animals?"

"For the jaguars and leopards. Not for the other animals."

"Not Kushna or Boo Boo…probably not lions, either. Just put on leash and walk to pen," Vladimir said.

"Why wouldn't you want to use the tranquillizer for all the animals?" I asked.

"Not necessary," Mr. McCurdy said. "And you got to remember that using a tranquillizer can be dangerous to the animals. I only like to use it when I have to."

I stared at my watch. "Nick and I better get going. I'll go up to the house, meet Nick, and we'll take off."

"Enjoy your dinner," Mr. McCurdy said.

"You eat with police guy?" Vladimir asked.

"His name is Martin. He was disappointed he didn't get to meet you today," I said.

"He wanted to meet Vladimir?" the Russian questioned.

"A lot."

Vladimir looked uneasy. "He come back tomorrow?"

"Do you want me to tell him he should, so he can—"

"No!" Vladimir said loudly. "I mean police busy people so no need to drop in. No need to see Vladimir at all. Go and get Boo Boo. Bear need to go for walk…Vladimir need walk."

"What was that all about?" I asked Mr. McCurdy quietly as Vladimir left the stable.

"Not really sure. He just didn't seem none too happy about that police fellow coming around here."

"I wonder why."

"Lots of people are nervous around police," Mr. McCurdy said. "Back in Russia I think it's different with the police."

"What do you mean, different?"

"The police aren't honest like they are here. I think they give people a hard time sometimes, take bribes, that sort of thing. That's probably why he seems jumpy."

"I guess that could be the reason," I said, although I had another sneaky suspicion going around in my head. Was Vladimir jealous of my mother seeing the acting chief?

❀

"I still don't know why I have to go," Nick protested, casting an evil eye at me. I'd told him on the way home what the "appointment" was. He wasn't happy with me, although that was nothing new. "It's not fair!"

"You're going, because Martin was nice enough to invite you. And quit squirming," my mother said as she took a wet face-cloth and rubbed away some dirt from his face.

"I don't want to go. None of this was my idea."

"Well," my mother said, looking in my direction, "it wasn't exactly my idea, either. And I'm going."

"Are you telling me you don't want to go to dinner with him?" I asked in amazement.

"I didn't say that."

"You better not, after what we talked about," I said.

"What did you talk about?" Nick asked, breaking free of Mom's grip to turn around and face her.

She looked as if she was trying to figure out what exactly she was going to say to him. Maybe it wasn't fair of me to have put her on the spot like that.

"I'd just mentioned to Sarah that I enjoyed my dinner with Martin and would probably like seeing him again."

"You would?" Nick questioned. He didn't sound pleased.

"Why wouldn't I want to? He's a nice man."

"There are lots of nice people in the world, but that doesn't mean you have to eat dinner with them every night of the week," Nick grumbled.

"Nick, two nights in a row is hardly every night of the week," Mom said.

"If the week started on Friday night, it would be every night this week so far. I know a trend when I see one."

"It's not a trend. It's dinner…two dinners. It's not a big deal."

"If it's not a big deal, why did you give Sarah a hard time about arranging it?" Nick asked.

"I didn't give Sarah a hard time—did I?" she asked me.

I shrugged. "Maybe a bit."

I wasn't thrilled about Mom dating, but I'd come to accept it. Nick wasn't that understanding. I think at some level he still expected Dad to come back. It was funny how the more time passed, the more Nick remembered their marriage as being a lot better than it was. It hadn't been good for a long time before Dad left.

"I guess I was just a little surprised, that's all," Mom said.

"You were surprised?" Nick frowned. "What about me?"

Mom ignored him, turning back to me. "What if you'd agreed to all this and I already had plans? Like another date or something?"

"I knew you didn't have any plans. I was going to make dinner for us, remember?"

"But you still should have checked with me," Mom said.

"And me," Nick added. "Especially if it involves me having to go along."

"I'm sorry. If I wasn't so busy with the buffalo, maybe I could have checked both your social calendars before I agreed to—"

"What time is it?" Nick asked, cutting me off.

Instantly I knew why he wanted to know. I looked at my watch. "It's almost six o'clock."

"Quick, turn on the news," Nick said as he raced out of the bathroom.

"Are you sure it's going to be on the news?" Mom asked.

"I can't be certain, but the helicopter was there. I figure an elephant chasing around a bunch of buffalo would be news."

"You're probably right."

Mom and I followed Nick. He'd already turned on the television to channel eleven and was sitting on the edge of the couch, converter in hand.

"I'm just happy that you two chose to tell me what happened this time instead of trying to hide it from me," Mom said.

The first time we'd made the news we'd tried to keep it from Mom. We'd even hid the newspaper from her, hoping that since we'd just moved here, nobody who saw our picture on the front page of the local paper would know who we were, and nobody would tell her. This time there was no point in trying to keep it from her. It wasn't as if the escaped buffalo wouldn't come up as part of the dinner conversation with Martin tonight.

"Even if it's on the news, it could be one of the last stories or—"

"And now for something completely different," the newscaster began. In the background over her shoulder appeared a bouncing video of an elephant, the three buffalo, and cars and trucks jamming the road. She disappeared and the whole screen was filled with the images. "Three buffalo escaped today from a private zoo operated by a local resident, Mr. Amos McCurdy."

"His name is Angus," I said.

"The news always seems to get things wrong," Mom said.

"Would both of you please be quiet?" Nick hissed.

"In an effort to capture the buffalo an unnamed boy—"

"That's me!" Nick exclaimed.

I *ssshhhhed* him.

"Used a trained elephant to try to force them back into their enclosure."

The camera zoomed in on Nick and the elephant. Nick appeared to be having a wonderful time up there.

"But as you can see, this was not successful," the newscaster continued. "Finally, with the assistance of the police department, the large and dangerous animals were driven back and secured in their pens."

The footage showed me holding open the fence, and the three buffalo running back in to join the deer.

"The only casualty of the episode was one police car," she said, and the camera focused on the cruiser sitting in the ditch. "It's believed that the officer driving the car when it crashed was the acting chief of police."

"I hope the police services board doesn't hear this and hold it against him," Mom said.

"What's the services board?" I asked.

"The board that's in charge of the police department."

"I thought the chief was in charge of the police department," Nick said.

"The board, usually with the mayor as the chairperson, is in charge of the chief, and it decides if Martin finally gets to become the chief."

"Oh, that's not good," I said.

"Many of you may remember," the newscaster continued, "that it was another animal of Mr. McCurdy's, a tiger, that escaped last year. One time was perhaps an accident, but two incidents of escaped dangerous animals? Perhaps there is a need for further investigation into this matter by both the local press and municipal officials."

"Oh, boy, that *really* doesn't sound good," Nick said, and I really couldn't disagree. The newscaster went on to another story, and Nick clicked off the TV.

"Don't worry," Mom said. "This is television news. The story is here today and gone tomorrow when something more interesting or newsworthy comes along."

"I hope you're right," I said.

"I just hope that all of this doesn't upset Mr. McCurdy too much," she said.

"The only way that'll happen is if we tell him about it," I said. "Remember, he doesn't have a television."

"Or a phone, or VCR, or microwave, or video games, or a CD player, or—"

"We get the idea, Nick," Mom said.

"So if we don't tell him this was on the news, he won't know."

"But what about the newspaper?" Mom asked. "You said there was a photographer there, right?"

"Yeah," Nick agreed. "It was the same guy that snapped that photo of me and Sarah and Buddha. You remember that picture?"

Mom shot Nick a nasty look, and the hairs on the back of my head stood on end. What a stupid thing to say. There were some things you didn't kid around about, and that was one of them. It was over a year ago, but I knew it was still a sore point with Mom.

"Well, at least this time it won't create any problems for Mr. McCurdy," she said.

"That's right. He's allowed to have his animals…right?" Nick asked.

"That is correct," she assured him. "Nobody will ever try to take his animals away again."

After Buddha escaped and was recaptured, the mayor had gotten a court order to have the animals removed. He sent in the chief of police, the captain—now the acting chief of police—and lots of other officers and the animal-control people to confiscate the animals. If it hadn't been for Mom fighting them in court, they would have succeeded. It had been the first time in my whole life I'd been grateful that she was a lawyer; grateful for us, the animals, and especially Mr. McCurdy. I didn't think he could live without those animals.

The phone rang, and I jumped.

"Sarah, it's just the phone," Nick said. "Take a pill or something."

"Nicholas, don't talk to your sister that way."

"I'll get it," Nick said, grabbing the receiver. "Hello? Oh, hi, Auntie Elaine!" It was my mother's sister. She lived on the other side of the country.

"Yeah, sure, they're both here," Nick said. "Sure, I can put you on the speaker phone." He reached down and pushed a little button on the base of the phone.

"Hello, Ellen, hello, Sarah," her voice crackled out of the tinny speaker.

"Hi, Auntie Elaine," I said.

"Hello, Elaine. It's nice to hear from you," Mom said.

"I thought I'd talk to you about your children's latest appearance in the news."

"You saw us on TV?" I asked.

"In living colour."

"How did I look?" Nick questioned.

"You looked like a kid on the back of an elephant," she answered.

"But a *cool* kid on the back of an elephant, right?"

"Nicky, how could any kid on the back of an elephant not be cool?"

Nick laughed.

"How did you see it?" I asked. "It was just a local television station's traffic helicopter that filmed us. How could you see it all the way on the West Coast?"

"It's probably just like that newspaper picture last year," she said. Great, just what I needed—somebody else bringing that up. "If a local story is important or interesting—"

"Those two words pretty well *define* me," Nick said, cutting her off.

"Or if a story is strange," she continued.

"Well, that certainly defines Nick," I said.

She laughed. "If it's any of those things, then it gets national or even international coverage."

"Are you saying they could have been watching us in Europe?" Nick asked.

"I can't comment on Europe, or any other continent, but I figure if I saw it here, it must have gone right across the country at least," she said.

I couldn't help wondering if my father had seen it. He was somewhere in the Midwest on a photo assignment, and we hadn't heard from him in over a month. Maybe if he saw it, he'd call.

"I just wanted to make sure you knew about this, Ellen," Auntie Elaine said.

"They told me about this one," she answered.

"There was also a newspaper photographer," Nick said.

"So perhaps if we're lucky you'll be in tomorrow's paper," my auntie added.

"If we're *really* lucky, perhaps we won't be," I said.

"I don't know," she said, "it's sort of cute to see my niece and nephew in the news. Don't you think so, Ellen?"

I had the benefit of seeing my mother's expression—something my aunt didn't have—and I knew she was far from amused.

"Cute isn't exactly the term that comes to mind," Mom said.

"Come on, Ellen, don't be such a stick-in-the-mud. I think it's pretty amazing that I've seen my sister's kids on the news twice as many times as I've seen them in person over the past year."

"Maybe that just means you should visit us more often," my mother countered.

"Life is busy," she said.

"If you come, I'll let you ride on my elephant," Nick offered.

"*Your* elephant?" Mom questioned.

"Well, it's *like* my elephant."

Mom gave him one of her famous looks—the one that could peel paint off a wall—that she saved for when she was in court, or talking about my father.

"I'm sorry if I interrupted your dinner," Auntie Elaine said.

"We're going out for dinner tonight," Nick said.

"What's the occasion?"

"We're going on a *date*," Nick muttered.

"You're all going on a date?" Auntie Elaine questioned.

"Mom's going on the date," Nick explained. "And me and Sarah are going along."

"Ellen, I know after being married for a long time you might be a little rusty about the rules of dating, but it's best *not* to bring your kids along."

"None of this was my idea," my mother noted.

"The dating part or bringing the kids along?" Auntie Elaine asked.

"The date was Sarah's doing," Nick said.

"You set your mother up on a date?" Auntie Elaine asked.

"Not really. She wanted to go out with him. They went out together last night."

"And you're seeing him again tonight? Two nights in a row?"

"Doesn't that sound like a trend to you?" Nick questioned.

"A good trend. Sounds pretty serious."

"It's not serious," Mom insisted.

"So, if the date was arranged by Sarah, who decided the kids should come along?" Auntie Elaine asked.

"That wasn't my idea. That was his idea!" I protested.

"*He* wanted the kids to come along? Now that sounds even more serious."

"Elaine, please don't make more out of this than there is."

"And just what does this not serious person do for a living?"

"He's a cop," Nick said.

"You're dating a cop?" Auntie Elaine exclaimed. "I remember you saying you'd never date a police officer."

"First of all, that was a long time ago—before I was even married," Mom said. "Second, I'm not dating him. I'm just going to dinner with him."

"Sounds like a date to me," Auntie Elaine said.

"And third, he isn't really a police officer. He's the acting chief of police."

"Even if he's the boss cop, that still makes him a cop. Is he good-looking?"

"Elaine, please grow up," Mom said.

"Me, grow up? I'm the one with a husband and three boring kids who never seem to make it on the front pages of newspapers or national news shows. It isn't me who's dating. Sarah, is he good-looking?"

"Well…" I glanced at Mom. She looked as if she was waiting for my answer. "I guess so. He's good-looking…I guess."

"All the better. I'll let you three go now so you can get ready for your date. And, Ellen…don't do anything I wouldn't do."

Chapter 8

Nick and I had cut through the fields and come up to Mr. McCurdy's by the back way.

"I'm going to go check on the cats," Nick said.

"Be careful."

"There's nothing to worry about, Sarah."

"Except for two tigers, a couple of leopards, a pair of lions, two cubs, a black bear, and a pair of jaguars."

"What could go wrong?" he asked. "I'm just going to give them their breakfast."

"What could go wrong is that you *become* their breakfast. Just be careful."

Nick chuckled. "Yes…Mother."

He cut off toward the barn and I continued on to the house. I pulled open the door and headed down the hall.

"Hello!" I called out as I hit the kitchen.

"Big girl Sarah, be quiet!" Vladimir hissed. "Angus still sleeping."

"He's still asleep at this time?" I questioned. It was almost nine in the morning. He never slept in that late.

"Late working last night. Angus need sleep. Wake later."

"Sure, that's fine." I was suddenly struck by a terrible thought. I didn't like even to think it, but I couldn't stop. Maybe he wasn't asleep. Maybe he was…

"Angus not dead," Vladimir said, "just sleeping. I check already."

I was shocked and confused. How did he know what I was thinking?

"Could tell by look on face," Vladimir said, again reading my mind. "Vladimir know Angus not dead by look from inside."

"From the inside? What does that mean?" I asked.

"When Vladimir little, maybe six, he have to watch grandfather while everybody else in family go to work. Grandfather very old and sick. He go to sleep always. Vladimir always watch for chest going up and down, hear sound of breathing to know he alive."

"That would be eerie," I said.

"Remember once when grandfather lie in bed and no move for hour. Vladimir think for sure he dead. Finally creep into room to get closer look."

"And he was okay, right?"

"No," he said, shaking his head, "that time grandfather dead."

My mouth dropped to the floor. That was probably the least comforting, most upsetting story I'd ever heard!

"That's awful! Was that story supposed to make me feel better?"

"Not try to make big girl Sarah feel better or worse…just story."

"But how do you know Mr. McCurdy is okay?" I demanded.

"Just look in on him only minute before big girl Sarah arrive. Angus making much noise like a saw cutting wood."

"You mean he's snoring?"

"Snoring loud. So loud if Vladimir's dead grandfather in same room he would sit up and no longer be dead!" Vladimir practically yelled and then began laughing.

I smiled, but now I was even more worried. That yelling should have woken up Mr. McCurdy for sure.

"Big girl Sarah want see something good?"

"Sure."

"Polly!" he called out. The parrot, who was sitting on top of the cupboard, turned to look at him with one big eye.

"Polly, come to Vladimir!" Did he really think Polly was going to come to him? Polly didn't even listen to Mr. McCurdy.

"You're wasting your time if you think that parrot is going to—"

All of a sudden a flash of colourful feathers streaked across the room and landed on Vladimir's outstretched arm.

"Polly, Vladimir's friend," he said.

"But…how?"

"Vladimir know birds. People say Vladimir has brain of bird."

I started to laugh.

"What funny?"

"It's just that calling somebody a birdbrain means that he isn't very smart, because birds don't have very big brains," I explained.

Vladimir snorted. "Watch. Polly, say name."

"Vladimir," the parrot said.

"That's pretty good!"

"Wait," Vladimir said.

"Vladimir is amazing!" the parrot said, saying each word perfectly.

"That's really something!" I exclaimed.

"Whoever say that bird have little brain is not very much smart. Birds smart. Parrots much smart. You know how many words Polly speak?"

"He says a lot of words. I just wish he could be more polite."

"Vladimir work on that. Watch." He reached into his pocket and pulled out a tiny bird treat. "Polly, look at big girl Sarah."

The parrot turned and aimed first one eye and then spun its head around and aimed the second eye right at me.

"Big girl Sarah is *pretty*. You say *pretty*!" Vladimir said.

Polly studied me with what I could have sworn was a thoughtful look on his beak.

"Girl Sarah is pretty," Polly squawked, and Vladimir gave him the treat.

"Wow, that's amazing Vladi—"

"Pretty *ugly*," Polly squawked loudly. "Girl Sarah is pretty *ugly*!"

"Hey!" I shouted.

"Still working on Polly," Vladimir said with a shrug. "Take time and many, many cookies, but will say nice things."

"Stupid!" Polly squawked.

"No call big birl Sarah stupid!" Vladimir snapped.

"Vladimir is stupid," Polly said, and then jumped off his arm and flew across the room, perching on top of the cupboard. I tried hard not to laugh.

"Maybe Vladimir has brain of bird, but not give up make Polly say nice things 'specially to big girl Sarah and Nicky and maybe big girl Sarah's mommy." He paused. "Ask question?"

"Sure, of course."

"Why not tell Vladimir that big girl Sarah's mother so *beautiful*?"

"You think my mother is beautiful?" I asked in shock.

"Most beautiful...like movie star."

"You think my mother looks like a movie star?"

"*Da*, like movie star. Father go away and not come back... right?"

"Yeah, he hasn't come back."

"Father must be man with a birdbrain to leave. Maybe Vladimir should not say bad things about big girl Sarah's papa."

I opened my mouth to say something in defence of my father but didn't.

"Mother wish to get married again?" Vladimir asked.

"I guess so."

"Marriage good. People need to be with people. Vladimir wish to get married, too!"

Did that mean he wanted to marry my mother? Maybe I was right and he really was jealous of the acting chief seeing my mother.

"Why didn't somebody wake me up?" Mr. McCurdy asked, walking into the kitchen.

I was relieved he'd interrupted this conversation but disappointed I couldn't get more information to confirm my suspicions.

"Thought you need sleep. Work hard yesterday," Vladimir said.

"I've worked hard every day of my life and today ain't going to be any different. Have the animals been fed yet?"

"Give fresh water. Food next."

"Nick's already down at the barn feeding the cats," I said.

"Good to know that somebody's working instead of sleeping or jawing!"

"What is jawing?" Vladimir asked.

"Talking, gossiping, wagging your tongue," Mr. McCurdy said. "Like we're doing now."

"First eat, then work," Vladimir said.

"Haven't you eaten already?" Mr. McCurdy asked him.

"*Da, da,* eaten, but long time ago. Need to eat again."

"Again! You're practically eating me out of house and home!"

"He's not the only one," Nick said as he came into the kitchen. "I just fed the cats the last of the chickens in your freezer. We need more."

"Me and Vladimir were talking about that. Figured I'd go today, and he'd come with me. That is, if the two of you are going to be around to watch the animals."

Nick shrugged. "Got no place better to go. Can I ride Peanuts?"

Mr. McCurdy looked at Vladimir, then they both stared at me. "Sarah?" Mr. McCurdy asked.

"Why are you asking her?" Nick demanded. "It isn't like it's her elephant."

"But she's in charge when we're gone."

"That's not fair!" Nick protested.

"Well, how about this for a compromise," I offered. "You can ride on Peanuts—"

"That's great, Sarah!"

"Let me finish. You can ride on the elephant if it's for a *legitimate* reason."

"Legitimate? What do you mean by that?" Nick asked.

"It means you can ride him if it's for a purpose and not just because you want to ride him," I explained. "Understand?"

He shrugged.

"Do you agree with that?"

"Sure," he said, and smiled.

I didn't like either his quick agreement or the smile that accompanied it. He had some idea up his sleeve.

"How long will you be gone?" I asked.

"A couple of hours at most," Mr. McCurdy said. "While we're gone, could you bring some hay up from the barn for the deer and buffalo?"

Nick nodded. "No problem." Something about his expression made me think I'd soon find out what his idea was.

❖

Peanuts dropped the bale of hay right at my side as I stood at the pen.

"Good boy!" Nick said as he gave the elephant a big pat on the top of his head.

I had to hand it to Nick. Not only could he ride that elephant, but he'd figured out a legitimate reason to do it. The bales were pretty heavy, and it would have been awfully difficult for Nick and me to drag them from the barn to the pen. With Peanuts' help it was effortless.

"Do you want me to get another bale?" Nick asked.

I'd been counting them as he'd been bringing them up. "That's the twelfth. That should be enough for today."

"It's no problem, I can get some more."

"We'd better save some," I suggested. At twelve bales of hay per day we only had food for the animals for another four days.

"Don't worry. Mr. McCurdy said he'd be getting some more," Nick said.

"I'm not worried," I said. "I just don't think there's any point in bringing any more than we need."

"Why? Do you think they might overeat and get too fat?"

"Funny, Nick, very funny."

"How about if I bring them up and we leave them here, on this side of the fence, until we need them tomorrow?"

"They're better in the barn. What if it rains tonight?"

"Then they'll get wet. Big deal. I'll just go up and get the bales and—"

"No!" I snapped, cutting him off.

"Why not?"

"Because I told you not to, and I'm in charge. But if you're really desperate to bring up some more, be my guest."

Nick broke into a big smile.

"But you can't use the elephant," I said.

"What?"

"You were only to use Peanuts for legitimate reasons. There's no need for any more bales, so bringing them up today isn't legitimate. If you want to get more bales, I'm afraid you're going to have to carry them yourself."

"That's not fair!" Nick protested.

"You better listen to me, Nick, or I'll make sure you won't be riding Peanuts again for a long time."

"Are you threatening me?"

"Not threatening. Promising. Think about it, Nick."

"All right, all right, you win!" Nick said, holding his hands up as if he were going to surrender. I'd really expected a much bigger fight.

"Take Peanuts to the barn. Then come back up here and help me break down the bales and toss the hay into the pen."

"How about if I get Peanuts to step on the bales so they'll be broken up? Then he can use his trunk to toss the hay into the pen."

"Take him to the barn...*now*."

Nick scowled but kept his mouth shut. He gave Peanuts a command, and the elephant turned and began to lumber toward the barn.

I took the cords off one of the bales and started pulling it apart. Grabbing an armful of hay, I walked along the fence. The buffalo and big deer had been hogging all the hay I'd already tossed into the pen, and I wanted my girls to get their share. They were still nursing from their adopted mother, but they had begun to graze, as well. All the animals—except my babies— ignored me as I moved down the fence. The two little deer shadowed me on the other side of the fence. Finally, certain that I was far enough away from the other animals, I stopped and stuffed a handful of hay through the fence. They greedily ate. While there was grass growing in the pen, it was obvious they liked the hay a whole lot better.

I heard the sound of a car coming down the lane and turned around. I wasn't expecting them back this early. Maybe they hadn't been able to get the chickens. A white minivan appeared, moving slowly down the bumpy lane. There was a lady driving, and I could see kids bouncing around—why weren't they wearing their seat belts? The vehicle came to a stop on the lane opposite me, and almost instantly the doors flew open and released a flood of children—there were at least six of them—and the driver.

"Hello!" the woman called out as she waved at me.

I didn't know who she was. Reluctantly I waved back as I slowly walked toward her. The kids were charging around, pushing one another and shouting, and two of them seemed to be in a fistfight. The woman did nothing. Either she hadn't noticed or didn't care.

"Can you tell me who is in charge here?" she asked.

"Me, I guess," I said.

"You?"

"For now. Mr. McCurdy and Vladimir have gone somewhere. If you want to come back later, they'll be here in an hour or so."

"Oh, goodness, there's no way I'm waiting that long. My son *insisted* on seeing the animals we saw on the news last night. My little Malcolm is just crazy about animals, aren't you, Malcolm?"

The one boy, who had been punching the other, stopped for

a second and looked at her. "Sure," he said, and then continued to pummel the other kid.

"He's gifted," the woman whispered to me.

The only thing I could see gifted about him was that he had a pretty good punch.

"Are these all your kids?" I asked.

"Oh, no. These are Malcolm's friends. This is his sixth birthday, and we were going to Chuck E. Cheese's, but Malcolm decided we simply *had* to come here instead."

"The elephant," Malcolm said without either turning around or stopping his assault on the other kid. "I want to see the elephant and ride on it like that boy on TV."

"That's not possible," I said.

"I want to see the elephant *now*!" he screeched. "I want to ride the elephant *now*!"

"Only people who have been specially trained can ride the elephant," I lied. "It's too dangerous." At least that wasn't a lie.

"Oh, dear. Could he at least see it?" she asked.

"My brother is just putting it away and—"

"There it is!" Malcolm screamed as he pointed down the lane. Nick and Peanuts were just getting ready to head into the barn but were visible in the distance. Before I could think to say another word, Malcolm charged down the lane.

"Hey, come back here!" I yelled out.

Not only didn't he listen, but four of the other children charged after him. The boy Malcolm had been punching stayed behind. He was probably grateful for the chance to have Malcolm focusing someplace else.

"You have to stop them!" I said to the woman.

She laughed. "I try not to put boundaries around his creativity," she said. "He's gifted, you know."

"Yeah, you mentioned that."

"We'll just stay for a few minutes," she said. "His attention span tends to be fairly limited. He gets bored easily. But here, this is for you." She reached over and pushed a twenty-dollar bill into my hand.

"What's this for?"

"Think of it as an admission charge to your zoo."

"It isn't a zoo, it isn't mine, and we don't charge money."

"Regardless."

"I don't want it. What I want is for them not to bother the animals. I've got to stop them!" I ran down the lane after them.

Nick and Peanuts were already in the barn and out of sight. The five children were racing ahead, closing in on the barn. I ran as fast as I could, but they disappeared inside before I could catch them. I just prayed Peanuts didn't step on one of them, but if he did, I hoped it was Malcolm. He'd become a gifted pancake.

"All right, everybody, get out of the barn right now!" I yelled as I ran in the door.

"What's wrong, Sarah?" Nick asked from his perch atop the elephant.

"These kids shouldn't be in here."

"I want to stay here! It's my birthday, and I'm going to stay here—"

"Shut up!" I shouted, and Malcolm closed his mouth. "Tell you what, because I'm such a nice person, I'll let you stay here for a couple of minutes. Then you have to go."

"I want to stay longer than a couple of minutes!" Malcolm protested.

"Either a few minutes or not at all. Make a life choice," I said to Malcolm. I walked up and stood right over top of him. I was pretty sure he wasn't used to being threatened—or made to do things he didn't want to do.

"Watch this," Nick said.

We all twisted to face him in time to see Peanuts bow gracefully—at least gracefully for an elephant. Whispering in his ear, Nick got Peanuts to stand, lifting one front foot and the opposite back foot off the ground. Quickly lowering those feet, the elephant raised his other two. It was pretty impressive. Peanuts then responded as Nick had him back up, turn, and elevate his trunk. I had to hand it to Nick—he really was doing incredibly well.

"Pretty impressive, don't you think, Malcolm?" I asked. There was no response. I glanced over. He wasn't there. Frantically I looked around. He was gone. The other four kids were standing right there. Then, suddenly, a bloodcurdling scream shot from the stairs, coming from the stable. It had to be Malcolm. He was down there with the big cats!

Chapter 9

Leaping across the barn, I barrelled down the stairs two at a time. I was terrified of what I might find if I didn't get there immediately. Malcolm was lying on the straw in the aisle between the two rows of cages. He was crying. That was good—you had to be alive to cry. Maybe the animals had frightened him. I ran to his side and pulled him to his feet.

"You shouldn't have come down here—" I stopped midsentence. The whole front of his shirt was in ribbons. "What happened?"

"That…that cat…it attacked me," he whimpered, pointing at one of the jaguars standing pressed against the bars.

"Attacked you? It's in its cage."

"It reached out…like this," he said, moving as if he were going to slap somebody.

Oh, my! I could see the torn shirt. Had it gotten him, as well? Slowly, reluctantly, I moved aside the ripped material and looked. There was nothing but a chubby little belly. No scratches, no marks. Thank goodness.

"You shouldn't have come down here. You're lucky you didn't get hurt!" I scolded him.

"My shirt is hurt," he whined.

"Come on," I said, hauling him up the stairs by the hand. It was like pulling an anchor—a chubby, gifted anchor.

"Malcolm! Are you all right, my darling?" It was his mother. She and the other boy had reached the barn.

"He's fine. He was just—"

Suddenly Malcolm burst into tears and began wailing.

"My baby!" she shrieked, pulling him up into her arms. "What did that horrible girl do to you?"

Horrible girl? Me?

"Hey, don't you call my sister names!" my brother yelled. He jumped off Peanuts' back. "She didn't do anything to your stupid little brat. Even if she did, he probably deserved it!"

"She had no right to harm my—"

"I didn't touch him!" I protested.

"Malcolm?" she asked.

"It wasn't her...it was a cat...it ripped my shirt."

"A cat?" She put him down and examined the rip he showed her. "A cat did that?"

"A big cat. A tiger."

"A tiger!" she shrieked. I could see where he got his attitude. "A tiger attacked my baby!"

"It wasn't a tiger," I said.

"My Malcolm wouldn't lie! If he said it was a tiger, then it was a tiger!"

"It wasn't a tiger. It was a jaguar."

"A jaguar? You have a jaguar here?"

"Two jaguars, two leopards, two tigers, four lions, and a bear," Nick said. "And if your kid's too stupid to know the difference, he's not very bright."

The woman opened her mouth to say something, but no words came out. I didn't know what shocked her more, a jaguar ripping the front of her son's shirt or someone saying he wasn't bright.

"We're leaving! Right now!" she said, grabbing Malcolm by the hand and starting for the door, the other five children trailing behind her. "You haven't heard the last of this!"

"We haven't heard the last of it, because you keep talking!" Nick yelled back.

"Nick, that wasn't very nice," I said.

"Maybe not, but it was true. Wasn't she ever going to shut up?"

I didn't disagree, but still. "I better talk to her. Maybe I should offer to pay for the shirt."

"Maybe she should offer to pay for seeing the animals."

I studied the twenty-dollar bill still in my hand. I could apologize and give back the money.

"You stay here," I said to Nick. The last thing I needed was for my brother to come along and say anything else. I couldn't control Nick's mouth, but maybe I could keep it away from her.

"Suits me fine. If I never see that lady or her bratty little kid again, I'll be happy."

I rushed out the door and came to a dead stop. The woman and her kids were standing in front of the minivan. Right beside them was a man—that photographer from the newspaper! Where had this guy come from, and how come he always managed to arrive at the worst possible moment?

The woman was flapping her arms and yelling, and Malcolm was crying and carrying on as if he'd been mortally wounded. Between their shrieks I could make out some of her words. I didn't like what I heard: "could have been killed," "dangerous animals," "my poor baby."

Maybe I should try to explain. Maybe I should just retreat back into the barn and hope nobody noticed me.

"There's the person in charge!" she bellowed.

I looked up, hoping Mr. McCurdy and Vladimir had just driven up. She was pointing at me! Now I *really* wanted to run back inside the barn and hide. But I couldn't do that. For one thing, my legs were shaking so badly I didn't know if I could move, and second, there was no way I wanted the photographer following me into the barn with his camera. Maybe I could straighten things out at least a little bit. The woman and the kids got into the minivan, and the reporter moved toward me.

"Good afternoon," he said, holding out his hand. "I'm James Jamison with the Bolton News."

Reluctantly I shook hands. "I'm Sarah—"

"Fraser," he said. "I know all about you and your brother and, of course, Mr. McCurdy."

I didn't like him knowing anything about me. Even more, I didn't want him to know anything about what was going on here right now.

"Would you like to comment on the statements made by—" he stared at the notepad he was holding "—Mrs. Amanda Sommers."

"I don't want to comment on anything," I said.

He began writing in his notepad.

"What are you writing?" I demanded. "I didn't say anything!"

"That's what I'm writing—that you did not wish to comment on her allegation that her son Melvin was almost killed."

"It's Malcolm. He wasn't almost killed! He didn't have a scratch on him!" I protested.

"But he does have a shredded shirt."

"That's his shirt. Nobody dies because their shirt got a little ripped."

"She claims his shirt was ripped—narrowly missing his stomach—by a tiger."

"It wasn't a tiger. It was a—" I stopped myself.

"If it wasn't a tiger, then what sort of animal attacked him?"

"No animal attacked him. It just ripped his shirt."

"Are you denying there are two tigers, two leopards, two jaguars, and seven lions in that barn?" he asked.

"There are only four lions!" I snapped. "And two of them are cubs!"

"So...you *are* saying that all the other animals are in

there…correct?" Again he began making notes on his pad.

"What are you writing now?" I demanded.

"That you confirmed all the other animals are there."

Darn! I was trying not to tell him anything, but instead I was telling him more.

"She also said the pens holding these animals are all sub-standard."

"She never saw the animals or their pens! She hardly even got into the barn!"

"Then perhaps you could show them to me."

"No!" I practically yelled.

"Are you denying me—a member of the press—access to continue my investigation?"

"No…I mean, yes. Yes, I'm telling you that you can't go in there."

He began to write again. I didn't want to know what he was writing this time.

"You should go now," I said.

"Are you asking me to leave?" he asked, sounding offended.

"It would be better if you left before Mr. McCurdy and Vladimir arrived."

"Vladimir? Who's Vladimir?"

I just kept putting my foot farther and farther into my mouth. I wasn't going to say another word. "You better go!"

"And if I don't go, will Mr. McCurdy and this Vladimir become difficult or dangerous?"

"They're not dangerous!" I protested. "Although Vladimir is bigger than that little car you drove up in. Now get going before I call the police and have them charge you with trespassing!"

He gave a weak little smile. "Fine, I was leaving, anyway. I've already got my story. You gave me *all* the information I need."

As he climbed into his car, I couldn't help believing that what he'd said was true. I should have just kept my mouth shut. This could lead to problems. I had two choices: tell Mr. McCurdy right away, or wait until tomorrow's paper came out and I knew how bad it was going to be. Then again, I guess I really only had one choice.

❧

Nick and I finished feeding and watering all the animals. Then I cleaned the kitchen and put some muffins in the oven. Somehow bad news always seemed easier when it was accompanied by food.

I heard the sound of a vehicle coming up the driveway. It had to be them. At least I hoped it was, because I didn't want any more unexpected visitors today. I grabbed the plate of blueberry muffins I'd baked—they were Mr. McCurdy's favourite—and started for the door. Maybe carrying the muffins outside to meet him was a little obvious. I put them down on the edge of the counter and rushed for the door.

Mr. McCurdy and Vladimir had already gotten out of the big rig and were walking toward the house. Neither looked particularly happy. I'd hoped to catch them in a good mood. Then again, maybe I was just being overly sensitive and was misreading their emotions. Why wouldn't they be in a good mood?

"Hi. How did things go?" I called out.

"Not good," Mr. McCurdy said.

Great, I wasn't wrong. I took a deep breath. In one long burst I explained everything about the woman and the kids, darling Malcolm, the ripped shirt, and the reporter/photographer guy. Then I waited. Mr. McCurdy didn't speak right away, and my stomach began to form an even bigger knot. I'd been in charge and I'd let him down. Finally he spoke.

"This boy…it was only his shirt that got ripped, right?"

"Just the shirt. He didn't get a scratch on him!"

"Good. But, you know, it would have served him right if he did get himself hurt. There were always kids like that hanging around at the circus. Thinkin' they're smarter than they are, and parents who are too stupid to act like parents and watch over 'em." I felt the knot in my stomach get a little bit smaller. "And that photographer guy, he left, right?"

"Right after I told him to go. He wanted to go into the barn, but I wouldn't let him."

"Good girl! I would've done the same thing! I always know I can leave you in charge and things'll be taken care of!" The last of the knot untied itself. "He's pretty darn lucky he listened to you and got the heck out of here before I got back."

"I told him that!" I agreed. "That, and that I was going to call the police and have him arrested."

"You call police?" Vladimir asked, suddenly sounding alarmed. "Police come here?"

"No," I said, shaking my head. "I only threatened to call the police, but I didn't. There's not even a phone, remember?"

"*Da, da,* remember," he said.

"I guess that's one of the advantages of having your mama seeing the chief of police," Mr. McCurdy said.

I didn't want to talk about that, especially if Vladimir was feeling jealous. "Can I give you a hand taking the chickens to the freezer?" I asked, trying to change the direction this conversation had taken.

"Vladimir not need help."

"It's no problem. I can help you carry some of them," I said.

"Not much to carry," Vladimir said.

"You mean you didn't get many chickens?" I asked.

"Same as always," Mr. McCurdy said, "and that's the problem."

"How is that a problem?" I asked.

"'Cause now I have eight big cats instead of one, so the birds he gave me will only last for one week instead of for a couple of months."

"Can you get more from him next week?" I asked.

Mr. McCurdy shook his head.

"Then what happens next week?"

"That's one of those things I'm a bit worried about."

Chapter 10

"I don't think you should show it to him," Nick said, trailing after me through the field.

"I don't have any choice." I had the newspaper folded under my arm.

"Sure, you do. You didn't show him yesterday's paper," Nick argued.

"That was because he was part of what was in yesterday's paper. Today's paper is all my doing."

"That's even more reason not to show him," Nick reasoned.

"You don't think he's not going to hear about it? You read what that guy wrote. There's going to be trouble, and Mr. McCurdy needs to know about it." I'd spent all last night worrying that the article was going to be bad. I was wrong. It wasn't bad. It was terrible.

"Fine. I still don't think you should tell him, but if you're going to be stubborn, could you at least do two things for me?" Nick asked.

"What two things?" I asked apprehensively. Knowing Nick the way I did, I knew never to agree to anything before hearing what he had in mind.

"First, could you show him the paper when I'm not around?"

"I guess. And the second thing?"

"Could you make it really, *really* clear that absolutely none of this is my fault…that it's all your fault?"

"Thanks for the support, Nick."

"Can you blame me? I'm always in trouble for the things I actually do without being blamed for things I haven't done."

That did sort of make sense. "I'll make sure they know you're not to blame."

"Do you know what would make this better?" Nick asked.

"No, what?"

"It would be better if you could give some good news along with the bad news."

"That would be wonderful—if I had some good news. What did you have in mind?"

"You could explain to Mr. McCurdy where he's going to get the food to feed all the animals," Nick suggested.

"You know how he's going to get the food?" I asked in amazement.

Nick shook his head. "No, but that's the sort of good news he needs."

"But the way you were talking I thought you knew where to get the food!"

"Me?" Nick questioned, shrugging. "I was just giving you an example of the sort of good news he needs. The newspaper is no big deal. If Mr. McCurdy can't figure out how to get enough food for the animals, then there will be problems…real problems."

Nick was right, of course. There were only enough chickens for a week and hay for even less than that. Where would the money come from to buy food?

"Are you going to show them the paper right away?" Nick asked.

"There's no point in putting it off."

"In that case, this is as far as I go," Nick said. "I'm going to the barn. You can get me when it's over."

I watched as he walked to the barn and disappeared inside. Now it was my time to go. I strolled up the lane toward the house and opened the door quietly. Maybe they were still asleep and I didn't have to tell them right away. I heard voices. There wasn't going to be any reprieve. Vladimir, Mr. McCurdy, and Calvin were sitting at the table, eating breakfast.

"Good morning, big girl Sarah!" Vladimir beamed. Calvin blew me a kiss.

"How are you doing this morning?" Mr. McCurdy asked.

"Okay."

"Just okay? Maybe you should have one of these muffins," he said, offering the plate holding the last one. It was nice to know they'd enjoyed them.

"I don't think that'll help. You need to see this," I said, extending the paper.

Mr. McCurdy took the paper from me, unfolding and straightening it out, then pulled his glasses down off his head. He certainly wouldn't need them to find the article. It was the whole top of the front page of the paper—a picture of Malcolm and his mother underneath the bold headline that read YOUNG BOY NARROWLY ESCAPES DEATH.

"That's not a good start," Mr. McCurdy said.

"What it say?" Vladimir asked, looking over Mr. McCurdy's shoulder.

"Why don't you read it yourself?" Mr. McCurdy asked.

"Only read little English. Read out, Angus."

Mr. McCurdy read the headline first and then started into the article. "'There was a near tragedy on the McCurdy farm when Malcolm Sommers, age six, was viciously attacked by a tiger.'" Mr. McCurdy peered up at me. "I thought it was one of the jaguars?"

"It was," I said. "I even told her it was a jaguar."

"Trust the press to always get things wrong." He turned back to the article. "'Malcolm, accompanied by his mother and five of his playmates, was at the residence of local resident Angus McCurdy. One of Mr. McCurdy's exotic pets struck out at Malcolm in an unprovoked attack. The young lad, celebrating his sixth birthday, had his shirt ripped from his body and escaped certain death by no more than a hair's breadth. Malcolm's mother, who was nearly hysterical, needed to be consoled by this reporter as she feared that her son's 'sixth birthday was almost his last.' Mrs. Sommers claimed that this animal was one of many, including an elephant, held in inadequate, unsanitary conditions in the dilapidated, run-down barn.'"

"Animals in clean cages!" Vladimir thundered. "Vladimir cleaned cages by self just yesterday!"

"She didn't even see the cages!" I snapped. "Neither did he. I made sure of that."

"Yep, you did," Mr. McCurdy agreed. "Which would explain the next part." He pointed at the paper. "'This reporter was unable to enter the barn to investigate these allegations, as he was ordered from the property by the person in charge, Sarah Fraser, age fourteen. Further, this reporter was physically threatened. Apparently Mr. McCurdy has hired a security agent, Vladimir, to deal with people who wish to investigate this situation.'"

"Why he know my name?" Vladimir questioned. "And what does this security agent mean?"

"I sort of mentioned it…I didn't mean to…it just sort of slipped out," I apologized.

"Security agent means you're like a guard," Mr. McCurdy added.

"Not good," Vladimir said, shaking his head vigorously. "Not good that Vladimir has name in paper…not good…not good." He got up from the table and seemed upset. No, not upset—scared. How could having his name in a newspaper be scary?

"It gets worse," Mr. McCurdy said. "Listen. 'This is the third incident involving Mr. McCurdy and his dangerous exotic pets— the second in two days. This newspaper is calling for a full public inquiry into this situation and the danger it poses to the general public.'" He looked up from the paper. "Not good."

"I'm so sorry," I said, fighting back tears.

"Why are you sorry?" Mr. McCurdy asked. "You didn't write the article."

"But if I'd handled things the right way, nobody would have

written the article!" I blabbered and then burst into tears.

Mr. McCurdy got up from the table and put his arms around me. I tried to stop myself from crying. I felt like such a baby—but I couldn't. He kept patting me on the back and saying, "There, there" as I sobbed and snorted and buried my face in his shoulder.

"Sarah, let's just pretend that you did do something wrong," he said.

"I did!" I cried. "I shouldn't have let those people go into the barn, I should have watched that boy so he couldn't go to the stable, I should have fixed things, and I shouldn't have talked to that newspaper guy!"

"That's a lot of should haves, but none of those were mistakes. Even if they had been, it's still going to be okay. So what if he writes some stupid things in the paper? None of that matters now, does it?"

"Well…"

"Nobody's going to take away the animals. Your mother made sure of that, remember?"

I nodded.

"So stop worrying. Okay?"

I sniffled a little and nodded again. "I'll try."

"Good, 'cause none of this stuff amounts to nothing more than nothing. You'll see. They're just trying to sell some papers, that's all, trying to make things as spectacular as they can. It's like the circus—make things entertaining for the paying public."

Just then there was a knock on the door.

"I wonder who that could be," Mr. McCurdy said. "Vladimir, can you go and see who—"

"Have to go to barn and check animals," Vladimir said. He ran to the back door.

Mr. McCurdy and I looked at each other. "I wonder what that's all about," Mr. McCurdy said as the pounding on the door continued.

"I'll get it," I volunteered. As I walked down the hall, I wiped my face against my sleeve, trying to rub away the tearstains.

I opened the door and froze. It was Martin. Behind him, standing beside a truck, were two men.

"Hello, Sarah. How are you doing?" he asked.

"I'm fine. What are you doing here?"

"Nothing serious. Just taking care of a little bit of business."

"What kind of business?" I asked apprehensively.

"I think you know," he said quietly. And, of course, I did. "There's been a complaint filed concerning the care of the animals and the standards of the cages that are holding them."

"You know the animals are fine!" I said. "You've seen them."

"Of course they are, but when a complaint is filed it has to be investigated."

"What do you mean investigated?" I asked.

"These two gentlemen," Martin said, gesturing behind him, "are from the city. One is with the Animal Control Unit and the other is with Bylaw Enforcement."

"What are they going to do?"

"One will check on the care of the animals and—"

"You know the animals are well cared for!"

"I know that, and I know he'll find that out. The other man has to inspect the cages to make sure they're strong and safe so the animals don't escape and pose a danger to the public."

I wasn't so sure about that last part myself. The pens were such a weird combination of bed frames, fencing, metal strips, and parts of old cars that they looked pretty strange. As well, if they were really safe, that little brat wouldn't have gotten his shirt ripped open.

"Don't worry, Sarah, everything will be okay. It's not that serious."

"If it isn't serious, why are you here? Why did they send the acting chief of police?"

"They asked for an officer to accompany them. I volunteered to go along so I could make sure everything went okay."

"What do you mean?"

"I didn't want Mr. McCurdy to do anything that might cause this situation to escalate. It's not a problem if he allows them to inspect and then leave."

"What if he just tosses them off his property?" I asked.

"Then the mayor will get more involved," he said.

"The mayor is involved?" That wasn't good news.

"He has a long memory. He still takes it very personally that Mr. McCurdy made him look bad before that last election."

"But he can't make Mr. McCurdy give up his animals because of the court order, right?"

"Court rulings get challenged and overturned all the time. What I do know is that if Mr. McCurdy won't let the inspectors do their jobs, the mayor will think there's something to hide. Between him and the newspapers, it could get really big and really ugly. I figured my being here would be in everybody's best interests."

"I guess you're right," I said, nodding. "Do you want to speak to Mr. McCurdy, or should I?"

"Might be better if it's both of us," he said. "Come on, let's go in." He hesitated at the door. "Is Vladimir around?"

"Sure, he's just gone down to the barn."

"Great. I've really been wanting to meet him."

Maybe he wouldn't feel that way if he knew Vladimir had a crush on my mother and didn't like him seeing her...at least that's what I figured.

We entered the house, walked down the hall, and went into the kitchen. Mr. McCurdy was still sitting at the table with Calvin.

"Good morning, Mr. McCurdy."

Mr. McCurdy furrowed his brow. "Morning. What brings you out here?" he asked suspiciously.

"It's nothing serious," I said, jumping in. Martin nodded in agreement.

"I see. So you just came to ask me out for lunch, did you?"

"Perhaps another time. Although I did have a great meal with Ellen and her kids last night," he said. "Did you have a good time, Sarah?"

"Yeah, it was fun," I admitted. He was a nice guy, and we'd had a good time, especially my mother. It was so nice to see her laugh. The only part I hadn't liked was that he'd asked a lot of questions about our stay at the exotic animal camp, the animals, and Vladimir. Maybe I was just being anxious when I didn't need to be, because those *were* pretty interesting stories.

"So if it wasn't to invite me to lunch, what brings you here this morning?" Mr. McCurdy asked.

"It's nothing to worry—"

"Sarah," Mr. McCurdy said, "let the man answer for himself."

"Have you seen today's paper?" Martin asked.

"Got it right here," Mr. McCurdy said, lifting it from the table.

"There were some issues raised that need to be addressed."

"Only a fool believes half of what he reads in the paper!" Mr. McCurdy thundered, slamming his fist on the table and causing the dishes to rattle.

Martin—he had insisted we called him that now—took a deep breath. "Do you mind if I sit down?"

"Suit yourself."

He pulled out a chair—the one where Vladimir had been— and sat. "I don't believe any of it," he began. "I have no doubt your animals would never be treated in any way that wasn't top-drawer."

"You got that right!" Mr. McCurdy snapped.

"So you let these two inspectors go out and—"

"Inspectors? You brought inspectors?"

"Two of them," he said. "One from Animal Control and one from Bylaw Enforcement."

"If they're wandering around my property and bothering my animals, I'm going to—"

"They're out by the car waiting," Martin said, cutting him off. "Nobody will do anything without your permission. You have my word."

Mr. McCurdy didn't answer right away. I held my breath.

"And if I tell you all to get off my property?"

"We'll leave."

"And then what?" Mr. McCurdy asked.

"Then the mayor and the papers figure you're hiding something. From there things could get more complicated."

"And if I let them look at my animals?"

"Everybody will see you're taking good care of them, and there will be nothing left for them to complain about. Well? Can we all go and have a look?"

Mr. McCurdy rubbed his face with one of his hands. It seemed as if he was really mulling this over. "What do you think, Sarah?" he finally asked. "Can we trust this fella?"

Trust wasn't something that came too easily to me, but I nodded. "I think you can."

"Fine," Mr. McCurdy said. "Sarah says it's okay. I trust her, and it looks like she trusts you. Let's go and have a look."

"It was a good idea to have Mr. McCurdy stay in the house," Martin said as we strolled down to the barn. Behind us were the two inspectors.

"I thought so," I said. Mr. McCurdy didn't have much time or patience for anybody who wanted to tell him what to do, especially if it had to do with his animals.

"Besides, we really don't need his help," I continued. "Nick's down at the barn, and that's where Vladimir went."

"I'd just like to lay eyes on Vladimir, so I know he actually exists."

"He exists, believe me! You can't miss him. Except for the elephant, he's the biggest thing on this farm."

"He's big? Funny, I had a picture in my mind of him being small."

"Vladimir's as big as a bear and covered in almost as much fur—long hair, a big beard. He's actually pretty scary-looking."

"Were you afraid when you met him?" he asked.

"Terrified," I admitted. "But you should have seen my mother's reaction."

"She was afraid?"

"More shocked than afraid. When Vladimir picked her up, gave her a hug, and—"

"He hugged her?"

I shouldn't have said that. This was crazy, being in the middle of this whole thing. I had to get out of it. "He hugs everybody. It's sort of the Russian way."

"How long has he been here?"

"I'm not sure. A lot of years, though."

"Well, the more I hear about him, the more interested I am in having a long conversation with him."

We came up to the barn. "Do you want to start with the cats, the bear, or the elephant?"

"The cats caused the problem, so that's where we should begin," he said. "And don't worry. Things are going to be okay."

"I'm sure you're right," I said, although my words didn't reflect the feeling deep in the pit of my stomach.

I led them around the side of the barn and in through the stable door. The stable was dark. I flicked on the switch, and the fluorescents hummed, glowed, and burst into full light. "Try to stay in the middle," I said, tiptoeing down the centre of the aisle. On both sides the cats sat in their cages—golden, glaring eyes staring at us as we passed, tails twitching nervously. One of the jaguars got up and slowly moved toward the front of its cage. I figured it was the cat that had reached out and ripped Malcolm's shirt. There was no way I was letting him sneak up on me. I backed away slightly. The last thing I wanted these inspectors to see was a repeat performance.

"Look out!"

I jumped as the other jaguar—caged on the opposite side—leaped forward and tried to grab me from behind.

"Are you all right, Sarah?" Martin asked, reaching out and stopping me from tumbling forward. He let go. My legs felt a bit shaky.

"He didn't touch me at all," I said. "You just have to stay in the middle and it's okay...safe." I looked from face to face. Nobody seemed very convinced.

"Sarah, why don't you bring me up to meet Vladimir and we'll leave these two gentlemen to do their jobs?"

"Maybe we should stay," I said.

"It's probably better if we have less people in this little space. Less chance of an accident happening. Be careful, gentlemen," he said to the two inspectors. They nodded in agreement. "Okay, lead me upstairs, Sarah."

I retreated to the rickety steps. Carefully I went up the stairs, with Martin right behind me.

"Hello!" I called out.

"Hey, Sarah!" Nick replied. He was sitting on one of the few remaining bales of hay beside Peanuts. "How did Mr. McCurdy react when you showed him the newspaper?"

"He was okay. There are other things he has to deal with."

Martin joined me at the top of the stairs, and Nick's expression changed to surprise.

"Hey, Martin! What are you doing here?" Nick asked.

"He brought along a couple of inspectors," I said.

"Inspectors! What sort of—"

"There's nothing to worry about," I said, repeating the words I'd been told but didn't really believe. "They're just here to look at the animals."

"Nobody's taking Peanuts away!" Nick said defiantly, standing up as if he could somehow hide the elephant behind him.

"Nobody's taking any of the animals away," Martin said. "This is just a formality. They'll look at the animals, say everything is fine, and then we'll leave."

"Are you sure?" Nick asked.

"You have my word on it."

❖

"I'm sorry we don't have any chairs out here," I said as I sat on one of the bales of hay by the buffalo pen.

"This will suit an old farm boy just fine," Martin said as he and Nick plopped onto two other bales.

"That's right. You said your family ran a dairy farm," I replied.

"Not ran—run a dairy farm. My father and his uncle still take care of the herd. They have thirty-five cows that they milk."

"I like milk," Nick said. "It's my favourite drink, although I try not to remember that it's really juice somebody squeezed out of a cow."

"It's a little more complicated than that. Lots of work being a farmer. Long hours, never a day off. Do you think a cow cares if it's Christmas, or your wedding anniversary, or your kids are in a play, or there's a big game where your son is the starting pitcher?"

"I guess your parents missed a lot of things," I said.

Martin smiled sadly. "I guess they did, but that's the life of a farmer. Probably a zookeeper, too. There's not a time when Mr. McCurdy isn't caring for these animals."

"He has Vladimir to help him." I wished Nick hadn't said that.

"Ah, the mysterious Vladimir. I'm starting to doubt he exists."

"Of course he does!" Nick exclaimed. "Tell you what, how about you and I go find him right now?"

"No," I said firmly. "I think it's best that Martin stays right here and watches what's going on." I didn't want him going to look for Vladimir.

"You can watch them, and we'll be right back—"

"No!" I snapped, louder than I had planned. "What I mean is, since we're here, anyway, we might as well toss these bales of hay over the fence for the animals to eat. I need your help."

"Sarah, can't we do that later?"

"Now."

"I'll help," Martin offered. "I've tossed a few million bales of hay in my time. I don't think a dozen or so more will hurt." He stood and grabbed the bale he was sitting on. Lifting it over his head, he got ready to toss it over the fence.

"Hold on," I said. "We have to take off the cords that hold it together."

"We'll toss them in first, then remove them when we go in and spread the hay around—hold on. We can't go in, can we?"

I shook my head. "It's best to stay on this side of the fence."

"I guess there are a few differences between caring for cows and caring for buffalo and deer."

"A few," I agreed.

He put down the bale, pulled off the cords, picked it back up, and threw it over the fence. The deer scrambled for it, while the buffalo didn't seem to notice.

"How many of these do you put in each day?" Martin asked.

"We've been putting in a dozen," I answered.

"At least that's what we're going to be doing for the next few days," Nick added.

"What happens then?" Martin asked.

"Then we don't have any more hay."

"None?" Martin asked.

"Maybe a couple of bales stashed away in the barn. I was thinking maybe we could use that big pile of straw to feed them," Nick said.

"Straw won't work. It hasn't got any nutrients in it," Martin said.

"Nutrients?" Nick asked.

"Food. Straw is just dried-up old hay that's only good for bedding. They don't get hardly anything to eat out of it. What if you just let them graze?"

"They've pretty much eaten everything there is to eat in their pen," I said, gesturing to the muddy enclosure.

"You'd have to move them to another pasture."

"You want us to move the pen? That would take a lot of work, driving in new poles and—"

"No, it wouldn't," Martin said, shaking his head. "You put in a few lines of wire—cattle fences, they're called—and the lines can be easily moved and changed to allow them to graze in new pastures."

"But how would a few lines of wire stop a buffalo from walking through it, or a deer from jumping over it?"

"Electricity."

"What?"

"A current of electricity runs through the wires, and the animals—"

"That would kill them!" I exclaimed, cutting him off. I thought of my poor little girls wandering into the wire as they rushed up to see me.

"It's a very mild charge, just enough to keep the animals away. I've touched them myself on more occasions than I care to remember. Believe me, it would work."

"But we don't have anything like that. Even if we did, nobody here would know how to set it up or use it."

"You have an expert standing right here. My family has miles of line. I could set it up and explain how it works. It's so simple a five-year-old could do it." He paused. "Well?"

"That would be great," I said.

"Now, if you only had an idea for feeding the cats," Nick said.

"They're almost out of food, too?" Martin asked.

Maybe we shouldn't be telling him any of this, but what choice did we have?

"They have enough for a week or so," I admitted.

"Do you have any ideas?" Nick asked.

"Not off the top of my head, but let me think about it. Maybe if we all sit down and put our heads together we can come up with an answer."

I knew I didn't have any answers left, but somehow I had faith that he might.

"All this talk about the animals eating has made me hungry,"

Nick said.

"You're always hungry," I said.

"No, I'm not," Nick protested. "Sometimes I'm asleep."

Martin burst into laughter. Great, somebody else who thought Nick was funny. "The inspectors must be almost done," the acting chief said, walking over to the fence. Hey, guys!" he shouted. "How much longer you going to be?"

"Not too much longer, Marty!" the animal-control man yelled back.

"He seems like a nice guy," Nick said.

"He is. He's an old friend," Martin said. "There's hardly a day that goes by that I don't bump into him. I've known him since we were in first grade."

"My best friend and I met in grade one, too," I said. "Although it's been a long time since I saw her. Not since we moved here."

"I guess it's hard to maintain a friendship from that distance," Martin said.

"We talk on the phone sometimes And there's e-mail and stuff," I said.

"It was difficult for my daughter when she and her mother moved away. It must have been hard to leave everybody you grew up with."

"No big deal," Nick said. "I just made new friends."

That may have been true for Nick, but I always found it hard to get to know new people. I missed my friends.

"When you live someplace your whole life, like I have, you get to know pretty well everybody," Martin said.

"But you don't know that other inspector, do you?" I asked.

"Not at all," Martin admitted. "He only moved down east a while ago himself. How did you know I didn't know him?"

"Just the way he was talking to you...or I guess the way he hasn't been talking to anybody. He doesn't seem very friendly."

"I think he's just concentrating on his job." Martin paused. "You're pretty good at figuring things out, aren't you, Sarah?"

"She's such a brain," Nick exclaimed, then suddenly seemed to realize he'd actually complimented me. "But a nerdy brain."

"I don't know about the nerdy part, but she certainly seems to know things," Martin said.

"I read a lot and I remember what I read."

"I don't mean just facts. You seem to figure people out pretty quickly, sort out situations." I wasn't sure what to say to that. "Speaking of situations, did you two have a good time last night?"

"It was fun," Nick said.

"Yeah, I enjoyed myself, too." I added.

"That means we know at least three of the four people enjoyed themselves. What about your mother?" Martin asked. "I'd be very interested in hearing if Sarah thinks your mother had a good time last night?"

"I'm sure she had fun, too," I said.

"Enough fun to want to go out on another date?" he asked.

Nick and I exchanged looks. "Maybe you better ask her yourself," I said. "You *are* going to ask her, aren't you?"

He nodded. "That is, if you two are okay with that."

"Why wouldn't we be okay?" Nick asked.

"I know that after my wife and I separated our daughter really didn't want either of us to date other people. I think she had some fantasy that somehow we were going to get back together again," Martin said. "Did either of you ever feel that way?"

"I guess a little," I admitted. I knew that was exactly how Nick felt. Maybe that was how all kids in separated families felt.

"I think a big part of it is about trust," Martin said. "You have to trust your mother to make the right decisions and trust the person she's dating not to hurt her. Of course, trust doesn't always come easy, does it?" He was right about that.

The two inspectors were headed our way. Maybe they were finally through.

"All done?" Martin asked.

"All done."

"And?"

"I've got no issues with how the animals are being cared for," Martin's friend, the animal-control inspector, said.

"That's good to hear," Martin said. "But I never had any doubts."

"They're all in good health, well fed. No issues."

I held my breath. Was Martin going to tell them we didn't have much food, or was he going to keep that to himself?

"Mr. McCurdy will be happy to hear that," Martin said, and I exhaled. He really was a good guy.

"But *I* have serious concerns," the other inspector said, and the hairs on the back of my neck suddenly stood on end. "The pens are completely inadequate," he continued. "The spaces between the bars are too large, the materials themselves don't meet standards, and in some cases they're just a collection of junk!"

"These are only temporary pens until Mr. McCurdy and Vladimir can build better ones," I argued.

"I understood he's had the one tiger for years," the man said.

"He's had Buddha for a long time."

"That pen is also not up to standards. I've been told he has a cheetah that lives in the house?"

"Yeah. But it isn't like you can complain about the cage. She isn't even in a cage," Nick said.

"My point exactly," the unfriendly inspector said. "That cat must be in an enclosure, and all the other enclosures must be fixed within four days."

"Four days!" I exclaimed.

"That is correct," he said.

"And if the pens aren't repaired in that time?" Martin asked.

"Then the animals will have to be removed."

"Removed! But Mr. McCurdy has the right to keep his animals. The court order says so!" I exclaimed.

"He has the right to keep animals in safe and approved enclosures. These are neither. I'm going to give him the papers and inform him of my decision," he said, holding up his notebook.

"No, I'll do it!" I snapped. There was no telling how badly Mr. McCurdy would react if the inspector gave them to him.

"Sorry, I can't give them to you. You're only a child."

"How about you give them to me and I'll give them to him?" Martin said.

"That would be fine," the man said. He handed the papers to Martin. "As long as he's formally served with the papers."

Martin looked at them. "Does it say here what changes must take place to meet the inspection codes?"

"It's all there in black and white."

"What if it takes him a little longer than four days?" I asked.

"That's all the time he gets. I'll be back to reinspect at that time, and if the changes haven't been made, the animals will be removed."

"Mr. McCurdy won't let you do that," I protested.

"He'll have no choice. I'll be here along with whatever is necessary to carry out the legal enforcement and the consequences of that inspection," he said.

"What does that mean?" Nick asked.

"It means the police and animal-control people," I said.

"But Martin wouldn't do that," Nick said.

"He won't have any choice," the inspector said. "Because that's what my cousin will order him to do."

"Your cousin?" Martin asked. "Who's your cousin?"

"The mayor."

"The mayor is your cousin?" I almost yelled.

"Yes, he is. And he's taken a personal interest in this matter. Anybody who's employed by the city, or hopes to someday become the chief rather than the *acting* chief, would be advised to do exactly what the mayor orders."

I glanced at Martin. His face was stony, silent.

"I better get going," the inspector said. The rest of us stood by the pen and watched as he got into his vehicle and drove away.

"I guess we'd better go tell Mr. McCurdy," Martin said.

"Not us. Me."

"But the papers were entrusted to me."

"I think it would be better if I did it by myself," I said.

Martin nodded. "You're probably right," he said, handing me the papers.

"Yeah, she is," Nick said. "Besides, you've already done enough to help. I guess we've figured out who we can really trust."

Chapter 11

Mr. McCurdy sat in the kitchen, his head resting in his hands, his elbows propped against the table. He'd studied the papers line by line, asked me questions, and then studied them again. Now he just sat there, staring at them as if he somehow looked long and hard enough an answer would reveal itself. There was only one way out of this I could see. I had to suggest it.

"Mr. McCurdy?" I asked.

He didn't answer. It was as if he didn't even hear me.

"Mr. McCurdy?" I called out louder.

He glanced up from the papers.

"I've got an idea."

"An idea? What we need is a miracle."

"We just need to fix up the pens."

"I don't have the money or the materials to do that."

"But you could get the money," I said.

"Get it how? You figure I should rob a bank?"

"You can borrow it," I said.

"From who?" Mr. McCurdy asked.

"From my mother."

"Yeah, she'd lend you the money," Nick agreed.

"I'm not borrowing money from your mother," Mr. McCurdy said, getting up from the table.

"Why not? She'd lend it to you. I'll ask her—"

"You won't ask her for money, and neither will I!" he snapped.

"But why not?" Nick asked.

"For one thing, I don't go asking people for money. Never borrowed money and never will, especially not from friends."

"But we're more than friends. We're like family."

"That's even more reason. Maybe things would be different if there was some chance I could make things work."

"What do you mean?" I asked.

"Sarah, even if the pens were okay, where am I going to get the money to feed all these animals?"

"Maybe we could borrow more money from our mom," Nick said.

"Borrowing means having to pay it back, and I don't see any way that's going to happen. Aside from a tiny pension that hardly feeds me, I've barely got two dollars to rub together."

Suddenly I remembered the twenty-dollar bill that woman had given me. It was stuffed in my pocket. I pulled it out...along with an idea.

"This belongs to you," I said as I handed it to him.

"I don't understand."

"That woman gave it to me. The one whose son's shirt was ripped. She gave it to me so she could see the animals," I explained. "She isn't the only one who'd pay to see them."

"Heck, I can't charge people to see my animals," Mr. McCurdy said.

"Yes, you can. Didn't the circus charge admission?"

"Of course, but this isn't a circus."

"No, but it is—it *could* be—an animal park. It could be!"

Just then I heard the door open, and Vladimir appeared. I'd wondered where he'd been. I was amazed at how somebody as big as him could keep disappearing. "And Vladimir can help make it happen. He knows all about this sort of thing."

"Vladimir know about what thing?" he asked.

"How to set up this place as an exotic animal park," I said.

"You mean like old Armstrong place?"

"Exactly! Exactly the same!"

"Could do. Could do, good!" Vladimir said, nodding enthusiastically.

"Then there'd be enough money to feed the animals and to pay back my mother for the money you'd need to fix up the pens."

"I'm not borrowing money from your mother."

"But that's the only way to fix them before the inspector returns and makes you give up the animals!" I pleaded.

"Give up animals?" Vladimir asked. "Why have to give up animals?"

In one long burst I explained what had happened.

"Bad...very bad," Vladimir said.

"It doesn't have to be. You borrow the money, fix the cages, then you and Vladimir make it into a park, support the animals, and pay my mother back. Simple," I said.

Mr. McCurdy started to laugh. "Sarah, things aren't that simple. What you're saying is nearly impossible."

"But not *completely* impossible. We have to at least try."

Mr. McCurdy didn't answer right away. That was a good sign. He was thinking about it. Just then there was a loud knock at the door.

"Who can that be?" Mr. McCurdy asked.

"I'll get it," Nick said.

"Sarah, let's just imagine that everything you said could happen—"

"It could," I said enthusiastically. "It could."

"Even if it could, I still don't know if we have enough time."

"That's why we don't have any time to—" I stopped mid-sentence as Nick, followed by Martin, walked into the kitchen!

"I just wanted to come back and offer anything I could to help," Martin said.

"Haven't you helped enough already?" Nick snapped.

"Nick, show some respect...regardless of whether he deserves it or not," Mr. McCurdy said.

"I guess I deserved that," Martin said, and I suddenly felt sorry for him. It wasn't as if it was his fault. "I just thought if there was anything I could do, I'd like to help."

"We don't need your help!" Nick said.

"It's just that Sarah and I were talking about the food shortage, and I had a few ideas."

"We've got all the help we need right here!" Nick said sharply. "Between me and Sarah and Mr. McCurdy and my mother and Vladimir."

"Vladimir?" Martin said. "Vladimir is here?"

"Yeah, he's right...he was right there." We all heard the back door close. Why had he run out? This couldn't be about my mother.

"Maybe Vladimir doesn't want to talk to you now," I said.

"Maybe nobody wants to talk to you!" Nick shouted.

Martin's face paled. He opened his mouth as if he were going to argue and then stopped. He looked hurt...badly hurt.

"I better get going," he finally said softly, and started toward the door.

"Can I ask you a question before you go?" I asked.

He stopped and turned around. "Of course you can, Sarah."

I tried to think of the way I wanted to say this. It was important I put the words together the right way. "Okay, what I want to know is this. If you were ordered to come here by the mayor to help them remove the animals, would you do it?"

"Sarah, it's not that simple. Things are complicated."

"I know they are. All I want to know is, would you help them remove the animals? Yes or no."

He took a deep breath and let out a sigh. "I'd do my job."

"That's what I thought. You were right. You better go."

"All right," Martin said. "There's nothing more I can say."

He turned and left, and I fought as hard as I could to hold back the tears. I heard the door close.

"What the heck happened to Vladimir?" Nick asked.

"I don't know, but he certainly got out of here fast," Mr. McCurdy said.

"Maybe somebody should go talk to him," I suggested.

"Somebody?" Mr. McCurdy asked. "There's only one somebody I can think of."

"You mean me?"

He nodded.

"Who else?" Nick asked.

I shrugged. "I guess I could talk to him."

I didn't know for sure that Vladimir had gone to the barn, but that was the logical place for me to start looking. Despite the hundreds of times I'd been in here, I still didn't like going in by myself, and the addition of all the new animals hadn't made it any easier. Maybe the inspector was right and those cages couldn't hold the animals. What would I do if a jaguar confronted me?

I peeked into the barn. Peanuts was off to the side, munching away on the last bale of hay we'd given him.

"Hello?" I called. "Vladimir, are you in here?"

There was no answer. Maybe he was somewhere else.

"Vladimir?" I said louder. "It's me." There was still no answer. I got an idea. "Come on, Vladimir, I hate being in here *by myself*…it's scary. Please come out."

Suddenly Vladimir stepped out of the shadows.

"He's gone," I said.

Vladimir didn't say a word.

"Can I ask you a question?"

"Big girl Sarah can ask many questions."

"I just have one." I paused. "I want to know why you keep disappearing whenever Martin comes here."

"I no understand what big girl Sarah mean."

"It just seems like you're hiding from him. Is it because he likes my mother?"

"It good he likes your mother. Could get married," he said.

134

"They've just seen each other a couple of times. Now all of this is going to make things more complicated."

"Too bad," Vladimir said. "It would be good for mother to marry so not be so alone."

"Alone like you?" I asked.

He shrugged. "Vladimir have animals and Angus."

"But wouldn't you like to have more than that?" I questioned, trying to let him know diplomatically and delicately that I didn't think my mother was interested in him, even if Martin were out of the picture.

"Have more than that…have girlfriend."

"You have a girlfriend?"

"*Da.* Pretty girlfriend."

"So you don't want to marry my mother?" I questioned.

Vladimir looked shocked. "No, no! Wish to marry Vladimir's girlfriend. Vladimir like big girl Sarah's mother, but not love. Love girlfriend."

My mind was spinning. "It's just…I didn't know you had a girlfriend. I've never heard you talk about her."

"Don't want to talk about. Make Vladimir sad to talk about."

"I'm sorry. Does she live by the Armstrong place?"

"Live in Russia. Not see for three years. Just write letters."

"That's sad. Is she going to come over here to join you?" I asked.

"Would like to join, but can't. Not now."

"Why not?"

"Can only come if sponsored to come to country."

"Why don't you sponsor her?"

"Only people who can sponsor are those who are—" He suddenly stopped.

"Who are what?"

"Nothing…no should talk…no want to get big girl Sarah in trouble."

"Please tell me. Does this have something to do with why you're always hiding when Martin shows up?"

"No, nothing," he said, but looked away from me.

There had to be some way to get him to open up. "Vladimir, you're my friend. A friend to all of us. When Martin comes around, you disappear and you look like you're afraid. And I know that you're not afraid of anything—not a tiger or a man. Please tell me what's wrong. Maybe we can help."

"If I tell, must promise not to tell Angus. Don't want trouble for Angus."

"I won't tell him," I said, hoping this was a promise I could keep.

Vladimir took a deep breath and then exhaled loudly. "Vladimir not supposed to be here."

"Of course you're supposed to be here. You were invited and—"

"Not supposed to be in *country*."

"What do you mean?" I asked.

"When first come, just visitor, and meet Mr. Armstrong. He give Vladimir job."

"I know all that."

"But not supposed to stay in country. Only supposed to stay for one month. Now here for three years. If police find out, Vladimir get sent back to Russia and Angus get in trouble for keeping me in country…if he know. You cannot tell him."

"But there must be some way to fix things," I said. "Maybe if I talked to Mr. McCurdy he could—"

"Big girl Sarah make promise. Speak to no one."

"You can't go on living like this, avoiding the police."

"Avoid for three years, can avoid forever maybe."

"How about if I just asked my mother and she—"

"Talk to no one. If people know, then Vladimir must leave. Vladimir want to stay."

"We want you to stay."

"Then big girl Sarah must keep promise. Will do?"

"I'll do it, but I won't like it," I said.

Chapter 12

"Mom, could you just come in and talk to him?" Nick asked. She was on her way to court and was dropping us at Mr. McCurdy's on the way.

"I can't speak to him about what you want me to talk to him about," she said.

"Why won't you lend him the money?" Nick demanded.

"That isn't what I said."

"Then you will loan him the money?" Nick asked.

"That isn't what I said, either."

"Now I don't understand," Nick said.

"What I meant was, I'd lend him the money, but he has to ask. I have too much respect for Mr. McCurdy to try to force him to change his mind."

"What about the animals?" Nick asked.

"Look, Nicholas, I'll give him a chance to ask me," Mom said.

"What if he doesn't? It's not like we have much time."

"The pens have to be fixed in four days...three days now," I said.

Mom didn't answer right away. "I'll come by after work today and I'll talk to him. I'll give him the opportunity to ask me, and if he doesn't bring it up, then I'll mention it."

"You'll come right after court?" Nick asked.

"Right after. I was going out to dinner but—"

"With him?" Nick demanded.

She nodded. "He invited me and—"

"You can't go out with him again!" Nick cried.

"I'm not having dinner with him tonight," Mom said.

"Good!"

"But that doesn't mean I'm never going to go out with him again."

"But, Mom, you can't go—"

"I can if I want. That's a decision I will make if and when he invites me out again. Understood?"

"I understand," I said.

"And you, Nick?" she asked.

"I don't understand, I don't agree, and I'm not ever going to agree, so there's no point in even trying to convince me that—"

"Oh, my goodness! What's happening?" my mother questioned.

I leaned forward in my seat and peered through the windshield as she slowed the car. People—maybe a dozen or more—were standing on the road in front of Mr. McCurdy's lane.

"What are they doing?" I gasped.

"Look, they have signs," Nick said. "It's a protest march! These people are here to try to help Mr. McCurdy keep his animals!"

My mother brought the car to a stop. "It's a demonstration," she said, "but they're not here to help Mr. McCurdy. Look at the signs."

As one of the marchers turned to face me, I read the big sign she was carrying. It read: ANIMALS BELONG IN NATURE, NOT IN A CAGE! I looked at a second sign. FREE THE ANIMALS! it said.

I climbed out of the car. My brother and mother did the same. We slowly made our way to the protesters. As we walked, I counted. There were fourteen demonstrators. Most of them were women, with a couple of kids, and one man.

"Do you know who these people are?" my mother asked.

"I've never seen them before in my life," I answered.

"They're animal-rights activists," she said.

"They're nuts, is what they are," Nick said.

"Nick, keep your voice down!" Mom whispered.

"Why, they're probably too nuts to understand what I'm saying. Look at some of those signs!"

I looked at the one he was pointing at. It read: PUT PEOPLE IN CAGES, LET THE ANIMALS LIVE FREE.

As we watched, one of the women came toward us. "Hello," she said, "my name is Rainbow."

"Your name is Rainbow?" Nick asked, sounding shocked and disgusted at the same time.

"Yes, Rainbow," she repeated sweetly. "Have you come to join our protest?"

"You want us to join you?" I asked in disbelief.

"We're here to protest the filthy conditions in which these majestic animals are kept and—"

"How do you know the conditions are filthy?" I questioned.

"Well, we read the newspapers—"

"You can't believe everything you read in the papers!" I snapped. "You should see things for yourself before you make a decision like that."

"We tried to see the animals," she said.

"You went onto the property?" I asked, afraid of what she was going to say or, more precisely, what Mr. McCurdy had said or done.

"We did. That man threatened us with violence. He said something about getting off his property before he got his gun! Can you imagine that?"

That sounded like something Mr. McCurdy would say. "I'm sure he didn't mean it."

"He sounded like he meant it."

I had to see Mr. McCurdy. I turned to my mother. "You'd better get going. You don't want to be late for court."

She looked at her watch. "You're right. I better get a move on. Judges hate it when lawyers are late."

"We'll see you right after court, right?" Nick asked. "You'll come and talk to Mr. McCurdy?"

"You can count on it. I'll give Martin a call and explain that I can't go to dinner."

"You don't have to call him," Nick said.

"It's only polite to let him know I'm not coming," Mom said.

"I mean, you don't have to call him, because you can tell him in person," Nick said. We both instantly saw what he meant. A police car had just pulled up, and Martin and another officer climbed out.

"I wonder why they're here?" I asked.

"We called him," Rainbow said.

"Why would you do that?" I questioned.

"To have that man charged with threatening us."

"You want to have Mr. McCurdy charged?" I gasped.

"He should be."

I turned to Mom. "Please, you have to speak to Martin."

"I'll talk to him," Mom said, and started to walk away.

"Don't forget to tell him you're coming right back here after court," Nick added.

"I'm going to speak to Mr. McCurdy," I said.

"You can't go in there!" Rainbow exclaimed. "He's dangerous! He could harm you!"

"You don't understand," I said. "He won't harm us. We're his friends."

"I thought you were here to join our protest to free the animals," Rainbow said.

"Free them? It's not like they're in jail, you know," Nick said.

"They're in cages! They should be free to return to their natural environments."

"How can you return them to someplace they've never been?" Nick questioned. "These animals were all born in captivity."

"But they should still be released into the wild."

"They can't be released into the—" Nick stopped mid-sentence. "But I'm not going to talk to you anymore, because you're a nut."

"Nick!"

"What, Sarah? Don't you think she's a nut, too? For goodness sake, the girl's name is Rainbow! Come on, let's go and see Mr. McCurdy." Nick began to walk away.

I glanced at Rainbow. "I'm sorry. He can be rude sometimes. He really didn't mean it...I've got to get going."

I started to move away. As I did, I looked back over my shoulder and saw Mom talking to Martin. I hoped she could convince him not to charge Mr. McCurdy.

"Excuse me," I said, inching between two of the protesters and after Nick.

"This isn't going well," I said, catching up to him.

"Not going well?" Nick asked. "I'm trying to figure out what could possibly make it any worse."

I knocked on the door, and we headed into the farmhouse and then into the kitchen. Mr. McCurdy, Vladimir, and Calvin sat at the table. Two of them were holding mugs, the third—Calvin—took a sip from the can of Coke he was clutching. Calvin gave us a little wave, but it seemed as if Mr. McCurdy and Vladimir hadn't even noticed we'd entered the room.

"Hello," I said quietly. They were both in the same clothes they'd been wearing when we left last night, and neither looked as if he'd slept. I hadn't slept much myself. "Are you two okay?" I asked.

Mr. McCurdy slowly shook his head. "We've been up all night thinking about ways we can get out of this."

"What did you come up with?" Nick asked.

"Nothing."

"Nothing at all?"

"Nothing that can save all the animals."

"But you think you can save some of them?" I asked.

"Calvin...Buddha...Laura...maybe Kushna."

"What about Peanuts?" Nick asked.

Vladimir shook his head. "Peanuts big animal. We sell and get enough money to buy things that—"

"You want to sell Peanuts?" Nick spluttered. "But that's what the Armstrongs were doing! What's next, do we sell one of the tigers, too!"

"Nick! You shouldn't be—"

"It's okay, Sarah," Mr. McCurdy said. He stood and walked over to Nick, putting a hand on his shoulder. "Nick, we don't like this any more than you do, but we couldn't figure out another way to do things. Between the problems with the inspector, no money to fix the cages or buy food, and now these protesters out there—"

"And Vladimir being in the country illegally—" I stopped. What had I done?

"Vladimir's what?" Mr. McCurdy said.

I glanced at Vladimir. "I'm sorry. It just slipped out."

"Had to find out sometime."

"It's just that maybe we have to find a way to make some of it work, even if we can't make it all work. Unless somebody else has a better idea?" I asked.

Nick shook his head, and Mr. McCurdy and Vladimir remained silent.

"Maybe I have an idea."

I turned around. Martin was standing in the doorway. What was he doing here, and what had he heard? I looked from face to face. Everybody seemed shocked and surprised—except for Vladimir. He was scared and started to get out of his seat. Was he going to make a run for it?

"Sit down," Martin said, pointing at Vladimir. "We're *all* going to talk."

Vladimir slumped back into his chair.

"You can't come barging into my house and ordering people around!" Mr. McCurdy thundered.

"I can and I did!" Martin snapped. "And you sit down, too!"

Mr. McCurdy folded his arms and puffed out his chest. Unless Martin was going to bring Peanuts into the house, there was no way he was going to move Mr. McCurdy.

"Please?" Martin asked, suddenly softening his voice. "I just want to talk."

Mr. McCurdy still cast him an evil eye, but he took a seat. I sat in the empty seat between Calvin and Vladimir. Martin took another chair and pulled it over to the table, sitting down beside Mr. McCurdy. I held my breath, waiting for him to begin.

"First off, I didn't heard anything when I walked in," Martin said. He turned to face Vladimir. "But even if I did hear something about an immigration problem, I'm a police officer, not an immigration official."

I felt the tension drain from my body, and a small smile broke through Vladimir's beard.

"From the little I know about immigration law, if somebody has been in the country a number of years, is employed, and has had no problems with the law, they are free to apply for legal status. All they need is a lawyer. Does anybody here know a lawyer?"

"Mom could do that," Nick said. "She'd help for sure, Vladimir."

"I not wish to be problem."

"It wouldn't be a problem," I assured him. "She's coming here right after court today, and we'll talk to her."

"Good," Martin said. "I'd like to talk to her, too."

"I still don't know how you figured you had the right to just come into my house like that without knocking or being invited in," Mr. McCurdy said.

"You're right," Martin said. "I had no right, and I have to apologize."

"Then why did you do it?" Nick asked.

"I thought it was the only way I could talk to both Mr. McCurdy and Vladimir—every time I show up he runs for the hills. This way he didn't have a chance to run."

"What is it you want to talk to us about?" I asked.

"Before I talk to all of you I have to clear up one legal matter," Martin said.

"What legal matter?" Mr. McCurdy questioned.

Suddenly it hit me. He'd been called here because Mr. McCurdy had threatened those protesters! "You aren't going to charge Mr. McCurdy, are you?"

"Charge me with what?" Mr. McCurdy demanded.

"You threatened those people, and they called the police—"

"Nobody is charging anybody with anything!" Martin said, cutting me off. "Although you do have to stop threatening to shoot people."

"Maybe if people stopped coming onto my property I'd stop threatening to shoot them!" Mr. McCurdy argued.

"I'm glad we agree, because that was part of the deal I made."

"What deal?"

"Those protesters really wanted you charged," Martin said. "But I convinced them I could only charge *you* if I charged *them*."

"Charged them with what?" I asked.

"Trespassing. They were on your property without your permission. As well, they were holding a demonstration without the necessary permits."

"You need a permit to hold a demonstration?" I questioned.

"Technically, yes, you do. Of course, nobody ever does apply for the permit, and we never do charge anybody for it."

"So you were bluffing," I said.

Martin smiled. "And you and Mr. McCurdy wouldn't know anything about bluffing people, would you?" I blushed.

He stood. Was he finished? Was he going to leave? Somebody had to thank him for what he'd done. He didn't start to walk away. Instead, he took off his hat and put it on the table. Next he undid his heavy utility belt—the one holding his handcuffs, nightstick, and gun. He removed it and placed it on the table beside his hat. Then he took the badge from his shirt and tucked it into his pocket.

"What are you doing?" I asked.

"The mayor called me into his office. He wanted to speak to

me about what's going on here."

"What did he say?"

"He said he expected me to personally supervise the inspection and have the animals removed if the standards weren't met. He made it crystal-clear that if I wanted his support to become the chief of police, I had to act to make sure the law was upheld."

"So you're quitting the police department?"

"Not quitting. Taking a three-day holiday."

"A holiday?" I asked.

"Yes, for the next three days I'm going to be here to help get things in order so you'll pass that inspection."

"And then?" I asked.

"Then I lead that inspector back in here to follow the letter of the law."

Mr. McCurdy smiled, but it was a sad smile. "I appreciate all you're saying. I really do. And I know you mean well, but I don't think it matters what you do or what any of us does."

"But we could try," I said.

"It's useless. No matter what we do the mayor isn't going to let his cousin pass us. He's going to find one thing or another that's going to finish us, even if he has to change the way the law reads."

"It won't happen that way," Martin said. "Because I won't let it. I know the law, and if you meet the standards, I won't allow them to do anything."

"The mayor won't like that," I said.

"I don't care what the mayor likes or doesn't like," Martin said.

"But if the mayor doesn't like it, he won't let you become the chief of police," Nick said.

"First of all, I want to be the chief to uphold the law, not to do what the mayor or anybody else wants. Secondly, if I follow the law, nobody, including the mayor, can punish me for it. If he tries, I'll sue him!"

"I know a good lawyer," I said.

"I don't know if I can afford your mother's rates," Martin said.

I smiled. "I can't say for sure, but I figure the cost of a couple of dinners might cover it."

"Are you sure she'll go for that?" Martin asked.

"I'll talk to her," Nick said, jumping in before I could answer. "She usually listens to me. She trusts my judgement."

Martin smiled. "That's important, you know…trusting people." He paused. "Do you people trust me?"

I nodded.

"So do I," Nick said.

"Vladimir?" Martin asked.

He shrugged. "Seem okay to Vladimir."

All eyes now turned to Mr. McCurdy. He cleared his throat. "Trusting you is one thing. You being able to help us is different. Unless you have some idea about how we can fix up those pens and how we can feed the animals afterward, all the trust in the world isn't going to do a thing."

"You're right, and that's why I've been thinking."

"You have an idea?" I asked.

"I have lots of ideas, but the most important of those is the one all of you already came up with—the one you talked to me about."

"What idea is that?" I asked.

"At dinner that night with your mother and brother you mentioned how wonderful it would be to turn this place into an animal park, a zoo, just like Vladimir ran before," Martin said.

Mr. McCurdy scoffed. "We're having trouble just hanging on to what we got without trying to build an impossible dream."

"I was just talking," I said.

"You don't understand. That dream is what will hold everything together!" Martin insisted.

"Even if we wanted to try," Mr. McCurdy said, "we can't even get the material to fix the pens we have and—"

Suddenly I was hit by an inspiration. "What about the materials at the old park?"

"The old park?" Vladimir asked.

"What happened to the cages, the ticket booth, the snack bars, and the other stuff?" I asked.

"Still there until property taken over by city," Vladimir said.

"Could we take them?" I asked. "Would anybody mind?"

"Nobody. I could take!" Vladimir said. "Take truck and go get!"

"How far is it from here?" Martin asked.

"About a ten-hour drive each way," Mr. McCurdy answered.

"Less...I drive fast," Vladimir said.

"Okay, about a day round trip, plus the time needed to take things apart and load them into the truck."

"It would be faster if he had somebody to share the driving and help load things up," I suggested.

"How about if I go along?" Nick asked.

"You?"

"Yeah. I can't drive, but I can help with everything else."

"Would that be okay with your mother?" Martin asked.

"I think it would," I answered. "You could go along, too."

"I think I should stay here. I can start to get the pens ready— I'm pretty good with tools—and there are a few other things I want to look into. Besides, it might be better if I stay around in case the mayor or that inspector or even those demonstrators cause any problems."

That made sense.

"There's only one thing we need to set this plan in motion." He turned to Mr. McCurdy. "I know it's a long shot, but do we try?"

Every eye was trained on Mr. McCurdy. He didn't answer right away.

"Nope," he said, and I felt my heart sink. "We ain't going to try...we're going to succeed."

I followed Martin and Mr. McCurdy as they moved from pen to pen. At each pen Martin would ask questions, check the inspection papers, and make notes. We'd started at the pen with the buffalo and deer. From there we'd checked out Peanuts and now were finally looking at the cats and Boo Boo. It certainly wasn't going quickly.

I looked at my watch. Nick and Vladimir had been gone almost four hours. They'd charged out of here so fast they didn't even stop to pack a toothbrush—of course, that would be fine with Nick.

I still had about three hours until Mom arrived. Three more hours to figure out how I was going to explain why I'd allowed Nick to go with Vladimir. Hopefully she'd understand, but if she didn't...so what? What was she going to do—chase after him?

"Okay, that's all the animals in the field and the barn," Martin said. "Now we have to decide what to do with your house pets."

"What do you mean, what to do with them?" Mr. McCurdy asked.

"The orders specifically mention the cheetah and your chimp. We have to fix something for them."

"There's no way in the world I'm ever going to keep Calvin or Laura in a cage in the barn!" Mr. McCurdy shouted.

"Nobody's talking about keeping them in the barn or a cage," Martin said.

"Then what exactly do you have in mind?"

"Let's go up to the house. It'll be easier for me to show you than to explain it."

We left the barn and headed for the house.

"How many acres you have here?" Martin asked.

"Close to two hundred."

"Are you working any of the fields?"

"I'm no farmer," Mr. McCurdy said.

"How would you feel about a farmer working some of the fields—renting them from you?"

"Thought about it, but there's not much money to be made."

"Maybe not much money, but how about a trade?" Martin asked.

"What sort of trade?"

"Let's say a farmer rents a couple of your fields and he puts in some grain and some hay. In exchange for working your fields he gives you enough grain, hay, and straw to take care of your animals."

"That would be great!" I said, answering for Mr. McCurdy.

"Do you think that could happen?' Mr. McCurdy asked.

"I was talking to a couple of the local farmers this morning when I dropped into the coffee shop—a lot of them get their morning coffee after doing their first chores—and I sort of mentioned I knew somebody who might want to make a deal like that."

"What did they say?" Mr. McCurdy asked.

"They were practically tripping over each other. If you want, I'll bring you there for a coffee tomorrow morning and we'll see if we can get the deal done."

"That would be amazing," I said. "Thank you so much! Now if only you could figure out a way to get food for the cats."

"Oh," Martin said, "didn't I mention it? I have that one figured out, as well."

"You do? How? What?"

He smiled. "Would the cats eat deer?"

"Deer? There's no way they're going to eat our deer!"

"Not your deer. Dead deer. Remember when your mother almost struck that deer?"

"Of course I do."

"Well, I was talking to my buddy, the animal-control inspector you met, and he was telling me there's a couple of deer killed by cars every week throughout the county. It's up to Animal Control to pick them up. He told me it would be no problem to drop them in here. It would make it easier for them to dispose of the bodies. Would the cats eat deer?"

"For sure! The cats would eat 'em, and those they don't eat right away I could store in the freezer for later."

"Good, then that sounds like two problems down," Martin said. We entered the farmhouse and walked down the hall to the kitchen. Laura was asleep on the couch. Calvin was sitting at the kitchen table. On his head was Martin's police hat!

"Hey!" Martin shouted. "Take off my hat!"

Calvin looked suitably embarrassed. He reached up and took the hat off, handing it to Martin. It was slightly bent out of shape and there was something—some sort of stain—on one side. "At least he didn't take your gun," Mr. McCurdy said.

"That is a plus, which of course leads us to our next problem. You have to have a cage for Laura and Calvin."

"There's no way they're going in any cage in the barn!" Mr. McCurdy thundered.

"I wasn't thinking about the barn, or a cage. I was thinking more of a guest bedroom."

"You want to explain that?" Mr. McCurdy asked.

"How many bedrooms do you have in this house?" Martin asked.

"Four."

"So that's one for you, one for Vladimir, one for other guests, and one we're going to convert to a special bedroom for your two house pets."

"There's no way they'll stay in one room."

"It'll help if you put in Laura's favourite couch, her litter box, that chair that Calvin likes, and—"

"And the fridge?" Mr. McCurdy asked. "That fridge is Calvin's very favourite thing in the whole house. He'll keep leaving that room to get himself a drink."

"Not if there's bars on the windows and the door."

"It don't seem right to keep them in a cage like that...just doesn't seem right."

"I only want you to keep them in that one room when the inspector is here. After he leaves..."

"They're free to wander the house as usual," I finished.

"Exactly," Martin agreed. "Does that seem okay?"

Mr. McCurdy nodded.

"So what do we do now?" I asked.

"I've got to get to town to take care of some business," Martin answered.

"I've got to finish feeding the animals," Mr. McCurdy said.

"I can help you with that," I added.

"You can do that after you finish a couple of other things," Martin said.

"What sort of things?"

"You're going to make some lemonade and bake muffins—Mr. McCurdy, Nick, and your mother all agree you make fantastic muffins."

"I could do that."

"After you're finished, you're going to take the lemonade, a bunch of glasses, all the muffins, and go up to the top of the driveway and offer them to the protesters."

"Why would I want to do that?" I couldn't believe my ears.

"Because they must be thirsty and hungry."

"I don't care if they're dying of thirst!"

"You're also doing it because you're a nice person, and because they're really not that much different than you."

"How can you think I have anything in common with some nut named Rainbow?" I demanded.

"She's not responsible for the name her parents gave her. Why do you think she's out there in the hot sun holding up a sign?" Martin asked.

"Because she's a nut!"

"No, because she has a true love of animals and is committed to trying to save them...which sounds a lot like why you're here."

I didn't know what to say to that.

"And finally, you're going to be nice to them because maybe, just maybe, we can convince them we really do all have the same goals in mind, and we might all end up on the same side. Does that make sense?"

I nodded. "What kind of muffins do you think Rainbow would like?"

"Judging from her name, I think something with a lot of fruits, grains, and *nuts* would be most appropriate," Martin answered.

Chapter 13

I walked at the back of the little knot of people that included Mr. McCurdy, my mom—acting as his lawyer, the bylaw inspector, the animal-control officer, Rainbow, Martin, the newspaper reporter and, finally, the mayor. I knew the mayor was only there for one reason—to try to make sure Mr. McCurdy failed the inspection. Boy, was he going to be disappointed.

Nick and Vladimir were nowhere to be seen. Partly that was because until the paperwork had come through—my mother had filed it with the immigration department the day before—we wanted Vladimir to lie low. The other reason was that the two of them were going from pen to pen, just before we'd get there with the inspector, to make sure everything was perfect.

"I'm so glad to be a part of this," Rainbow said quietly to me.

"After all the work you and your friends did to help, you deserve to be here."

"It was just so wonderful to be part of saving these magnificent animals," she said.

Rainbow and a few of the other protesters had worked as hard as anybody over the past two days to get the farm in shape. Once they understood that if Mr. McCurdy failed the inspection, the animals wouldn't be freed—they'd be killed—they decided to help make things work. Martin had been right about them loving animals. Actually Martin had been right about a lot of things.

My mother stopped at the door to the stable. "Before we allow you to start this inspection—"

"You should realize you have no choice but to allow this inspection!" the mayor said, cutting her off.

"And you should realize you're simply a guest...here only because Mr. McCurdy has allowed you to be."

"I'm the mayor!"

"I don't care if you're the queen of England," my mother countered. "You have no authority to be here on private property."

"As the mayor I have—"

"No authority to be here," my mother said firmly. "Perhaps you might want to check with the acting chief."

The mayor stared at Martin. "Well?"

"I'm afraid she's correct. The only people who have the authority to be here are the two inspectors. Technically they could ask me to leave, as well."

"I think it's essential the chief be here. You wouldn't do that...would you...ask the chief to leave?" the mayor asked. He suddenly didn't sound so confident.

"He can stay," Mr. McCurdy said.

The mayor smiled, and the tension on his face seemed to dissolve.

"But you're a different matter," my mother said, looking directly at the mayor. "So I'd mind my manners, or I'll ask the police to have you removed."

The mayor remained silent while others among us tried to stifle laughter.

"Now that we all agree on those points," my mother said, "I want to make a statement for the press." The reporter pulled out his pad. "We welcome the press, inspectors, and the public. We've made every effort to bring all parts of this operation up to the standards established by the municipal bylaws...and believe me, I'm completely familiar with each of the bylaws."

"As are our inspectors," the mayor said.

"Excellent. Then there will be no confusion," my mother continued, "because I'm also very familiar with the difference between an inspection and harassment."

"Are you implying we're harassing your client?" the mayor asked.

"I'm implying nothing. I'm stating that I know the difference between the *law* and a *lawsuit* and would be prepared to launch the latter if the former isn't followed."

The mayor didn't answer. He didn't look nearly as smug or happy as he had before. "Please, let's get on with the inspection," he finally said.

We all filed into the barn, one after the other. It was brightly lit—all the fluorescent lights were glowing. The floor was clean and bare. Strangest of all was the smell. The barn smelled like fresh flowers, courtesy of two whole cans of air freshener. The stables along both walls had been replaced with the specially fitted mesh and bars that had made up the cages and enclosures at the Armstrong animal farm.

The two inspectors went to the cage. One pulled out a tape measure and began measuring the bars. The mayor, my mother, and Martin stood right behind the two of them, peering over their shoulders. I retreated to the far side of the barn where I could watch but keep some distance from the action. Along the wall there were hundreds of bales of hay—part of the deal Martin had arranged between Mr. McCurdy and the farmer who was going to plant two of his fields. Rainbow came over and stood beside me.

"It really looks good in here," she whispered.

"Really good."

"Do you think it's going to take a long time?"

"I'm worried it's going to take as long as they need to find something wrong," I said under my breath.

"We might as well make ourselves comfortable," Rainbow said

as she sat on one of the bales of hay. I sat beside her. I could watch just as easily sitting as I could standing. Besides, with Martin and my mother right there, they'd make sure things went the right way.

🐾

"We're finished here," the bylaw-enforcement officer said.

"And?" my mother asked.

"We should go and inspect the pen holding the buffalo and deer."

"But what about this area?" my mother persisted.

"I'm finished with this area."

"I understand that. Did it pass the inspection?"

"Yes, I would think there's no need to look further if these pens are unsatisfactory," the mayor said.

The inspector scowled and didn't answer right away. Did that mean he was just waiting, savouring the bad news and then—

"They're fine," he said softly.

"They passed the inspection?" the mayor demanded, sounding shocked.

The inspector nodded.

"Fantastic!" my mother exclaimed.

Rainbow and I exchanged high fives.

"So we've passed the inspection?" my mother asked.

"You've passed the *first* part of the inspection."

"Therefore, there are no grounds for the removal of any of these animals," my mother stated.

That meant Buddha, Kushna, the leopards, lions, jaguars, and Boo Boo were all okay—nobody could take them away. I looked at Mr. McCurdy. For the very first time I saw a little smile appear on his face.

"There are still other animals to be inspected," the bylaw inspector answered.

"I suggest we go around to the front of the barn where you

can look at the new enclosure that's been constructed for the elephant."

"You built a new enclosure?" the mayor asked.

"We built new enclosures for all the animals," my mother answered.

The mayor didn't seem happy. Mr. McCurdy started to giggle, and my mother shot him a dirty look. He stopped. Before anybody arrived, my mother had warned Mr. McCurdy that he was to do nothing to insult the mayor or make fun of him.

"Please follow me, gentlemen," my mother said, and the parade of people filed out of the stable. I watched them walk off and then quickly moved back the other way to the rickety old steps running up to the main level. I took the stairs two at a time. I needed to get upstairs before they did to warn Vladimir and Nick they were coming. The two needed to get out of there, out of sight, and up to the deer enclosure.

"Nick! Vladimir!" I called out as I reached the top of the stairs.

They stepped out of the shadows. Peanuts was standing in the big doorway, partway out and partway in the barn.

"They're coming. You two have to get up to the deer pen."

"We were trying to listen," Nick said. "How did it go?"

"The pens passed the inspection," I said.

"Fantastic!" Nick yelled, and Vladimir picked him up and spun him around.

"Can you two save your little celebration dance until it's all over? You have to get out of here fast before they come!"

Vladimir put Nick down. They both headed for the big door.

"Not that way!" I yelled. "Go down the stairs and circle around the barn—really wide—so they don't see you."

I started back down the stairs, and they were practically riding on my heels. I ran for the stable door, trying to catch up to the group. I didn't want to miss anything that was going to happen.

"Sarah!" Nick called out, and I skidded to a stop and turned around. "Sarah...take care of Peanuts."

"He's okay, isn't he?"

"I mean, don't let them take Peanuts away," Nick said.

"He'll be fine."

"Promise?"

"You want me to promise you he'll be okay?" I questioned. Nick shook his head.

"But I don't know if his pen will pass the inspection," I pleaded. "I can't guarantee that."

"I don't want you to guarantee it. I want you to promise that if it fails the inspection you'll come up with something to save him, something that'll stop them from taking away my elephant."

"But, Nick, I don't know if I can do that."

"Sure you can, Sarah. You always think of something. That's why I trust you so much," he said.

"Yeah, right, so what's the punch line?" I asked, not expecting a compliment from my brother.

"No punch line. I do trust you. Please, promise me."

"If it fails the inspection, I don't know what I can do."

"You'll think of something, Sarah. Just have as much faith in yourself as I do. Promise?"

"Okay...I promise. Now get going!"

Nick and Vladimir circled around the barn in one way—they were going to take a route through the forest to stay under the cover of the trees—and I ran around the other direction to catch up to everyone else. I caught up to the group just as they reached the fence surrounding the outside part of Peanuts' enclosure.

"This little fence is hardly high enough to contain an elephant," the mayor said. "We can't have it rampaging along our roads anymore."

"I don't believe it ever was rampaging along the roads," my mother said. "And that little fence is certainly high enough. You see, elephants aren't noted for their ability to jump over things."

"Jumping isn't involved. He could just step over it," the mayor said. "Wouldn't you agree?" he asked the inspector.

Before the inspector could speak, my mother jumped in. "It doesn't matter what he *thinks* because we *know*. This fence was built to the specifications supplied by the National Zoo, and here are the papers to prove it. Would you like to see them?"

Without saying a word the inspector reached out, took them from her, and began flipping through them.

"Regardless of the height, what's to stop the elephant from simply smashing through that fence? It certainly doesn't look that strong," the mayor said.

"Two things," my mother said. "Those posts are driven into the ground almost three feet. And you might notice the small strand of wire extending along the fence. It's electrified wire."

"You mean like they use to contain cattle?" the mayor asked. "But could that control an elephant?"

"I'm certain it would be effective," the animal-control officer— Martin's good friend—said. He'd been here a lot over the past three days helping, and I knew he'd say nothing to hurt us.

"Well," the mayor said, "is the electricity turned on?"

"Why don't you reach down and touch it to find out?" Mr. McCurdy suggested under his breath. My mother shot him a dirty look.

The mayor didn't say a word. Either he didn't hear Mr. McCurdy, chose to ignore him, or just didn't understand exactly what he had meant.

"I can't help but notice how you've made this pen very livable for the animal," the animal-control officer said.

"We've spent a lot of time and effort to do that," Mr. McCurdy answered.

"What are those two poles for?" the bylaw inspector asked. He was referring to two tall poles, even taller than Peanuts. There were two bales of hay tied to the top of each of them.

"Elephants are used to reaching up to get leaves from trees. This makes it similar," Mr. McCurdy said.

"Wasn't that pond filled with filthy water when I was here for the original inspection?" the inspector asked.

"Yes, it was," my mother confirmed. "But as you can tell, it's now clean and fresh. So fresh you could drink from it."

What my mother didn't explain was how it got clean. Martin had arranged for one of his friends—the fire chief—to send over one of his pumper trucks. The firemen had used the truck and hoses to drain the whole pond and then refill it from the creek. Martin had explained that the fire chief didn't like the mayor any more than he did, and was happy to help out.

Mr. McCurdy had told us there was a little spring at the bottom of the pond. Between the spring and rainwater, if all went well, it might stay clean.

I couldn't help but think what the mayor would do if he found out what his fire department had done, but Martin had told me it was "covered." Apparently the fire chief had listed it in the log as a training exercise for his pump crew and just hadn't written down where the "exercise" took place. Actually Martin had arranged for a whole lot of his friends and fellow city employees to come and help. People from the power company came and hooked up lines to supply the electrical fences, a works department crew drove the poles into the ground for Peanuts' enclosure, and clerks down at city hall made sure we got some of the special papers and permits we'd needed.

There were the other people who had helped: Rainbow and the other protesters; two guys from the lumber company who donated wood and materials; and the farmer who had brought over grain and hay in exchange for the fields he was going to work next spring.

"You'll find this pen to be in perfect shape," my mother said. "You'll find that all the pens are not only able to pass this bylaw inspection but are up to the standards established by zoos across the country. And we've done that for a very special reason." She paused and then slowly turned to me. "Sarah, can you do the unveiling?"

I walked over to the shed that sat just outside Peanuts' enclosure. A gigantic tarp covered the entire side of the small building. I reached up and pulled it away to reveal brilliant, newly painted letters that read TIGER TOWN.

"Tiger town?" the mayor questioned. "What exactly does that mean?"

"It's the name of the newest tourist attraction in the county, an exotic animal sanctuary!" I said.

The mayor opened his mouth as if he wanted to say something, but he just sputtered and no words came out.

"We've invited a member of our local newspaper here so he could be the first to break the story to the world," Mom said. "The park will be open to the public on Saturday, and the admission will be—"

"Admission to the park!" the mayor thundered. "You can't simply open a business like a bunch of kids operating a lemonade stand! There are forms that must be filled in, permission that must be granted, bylaws to satisfy!"

My mother smiled. She removed a sheaf of papers from her briefcase and handed them to him. "You'll find everything that's required."

He stared at the papers, glassy-eyed, as if he couldn't read them or, more likely, couldn't believe them.

"Furthermore, we've listed Tiger Town with the Better Business Bureau, and Mr. McCurdy has joined the local Chamber of Commerce," my mother said.

"The Chamber of Commerce...my Chamber of Commerce... the one I'm the president of?" the mayor asked in disbelief.

"One and the same," my mother said. "And we certainly hope that you, as both the mayor and the president of the Chamber of Commerce, will be here Saturday for the official opening of the park."

"Yeah, we were sort of hoping you'd cut the ribbon to open the place," Mr. McCurdy said.

"You . . .you…must be joking," he stammered.

"No," my mother said, shaking her head. "We anticipated you'd want to be here. There'll be members of the press and a whole lot of people. We thought it would be better if all the people who support this place see you as a friend."

The mayor puffed out his chest. "Do you think you can get me to change my mind because of the promise of a few votes?"

"Seven hundred and ninety-two votes," my mother said.

"Seven hundred votes?" the mayor questioned.

"Seven hundred and ninety-two. That's the number of people who have already paid for a season's pass to the park. They're certainly not going to be happy with you if you try to close down the place."

The mayor glared and scowled—and then his face softened. "What time do you want me to be here to cut the ribbon?"

Suddenly everybody started to cheer. Vladimir picked me up and swung me around, Mr. McCurdy began pumping the mayor's hand as if he were his oldest friend in the world, and even the bylaw inspector cracked a smile. Tiger Town was going to happen! It was going to happen! This was just the beginning of something incredible and wonderful.

Then I saw my mother give Martin a great big kiss right on the lips. Wow…maybe this was the start of a whole lot of things!